Tennessee Williams (1911–83) started writing plays and publishing poetry while holding a variety of odd jobs. His first real recognition came in 1940, when he received a Rockefeller fellowship. Soon, *The Glass Menagerie* (1944) established him as a leading American playwright. Among his major plays, which have been turned into movies, operas, ballets, and television programs, are *A Streetcar Named Desire* (1947), for which he won his first Pulitzer Prize; *Summer and Smoke* (1948); *Sweet Bird of Youth* (1959); and *The Night of the Iguana* (1961). He received a second Pulitzer Prize for *Cat on a Hot Tin Roof* (1955). Among other honors, Williams received the Gold Medal for Literature from the American Academy of Arts and Letters and the National Institute of Arts and Letters.

CAT ON A HOT TIN ROOF

Tennessee Williams

And you, my father, there on the sad height,
Curse, bless, me now with your fierce tears, I pray.
Do not go gentle into that good night.
Rage, rage against the dying of the light!

DYLAN THOMAS

A SIGNET BOOK

SIGNET
Published by New American Library, a division of
Penguin Group (USA) Inc., 375 Hudson Street,
New York, New York 10014, USA
Penguin Group (Canada), 90 Eglinton Avenue East, Suite 700, Toronto,
Ontario M4P 2Y3, Canada (a division of Pearson Penguin Canada Inc.)
Penguin Books Ltd., 80 Strand, London WC2R 0RL, England
Penguin Ireland, 25 St. Stephen's Green, Dublin 2,
Ireland (a division of Penguin Books Ltd.)
Penguin Group (Australia), 250 Camberwell Road, Camberwell, Victoria 3124,
Australia (a division of Pearson Australia Group Pty. Ltd.)
Penguin Books India Pvt. Ltd., 11 Community Centre, Panchsheel Park,
New Delhi - 110 017, India
Penguin Group (NZ), cnr Airborne and Rosedale Roads, Albany,
Auckland 1310, New Zealand (a division of Pearson New Zealand Ltd.)
Penguin Books (South Africa) (Pty.) Ltd., 24 Sturdee Avenue,
Rosebank, Johannesburg 2196, South Africa

Penguin Books Ltd., Registered Offices:
80 Strand, London WC2R 0RL, England

Published by Signet, an imprint of New American Library, a division of Penguin
Group (USA) Inc. This is an authorized reprint of a hardcover edition published
by New Directions.

First Signet Printing, September 1958
60   59   58   57   56

Copyright The University of the South, 1954, 1955
Copyright © renewed The University of the South, 1982, 1983
All rights reserved, including the right of reproduction in whole or in part in
any form.

(Performance rights and acknowledgments can be found on page 175.)

Printed in the United States of America

PERSON—TO—PERSON

Of course it is a pity that so much of all creative work is so closely related to the personality of the one who does it.

It is sad and embarrassing and unattractive that those emotions that stir him deeply enough to demand expression, and to charge their expression with some measure of light and power, are nearly all rooted, however changed in their surface, in the particular and sometimes peculiar concerns of the artist himself, that special world, the passions and images of it that each of us weaves about him from birth to death, a web of monstrous complexity, spun forth at a speed that is incalculable to a length beyond measure, from the spider mouth of his own singular perceptions.

It is a lonely idea, a lonely condition, so terrifying to think of that we usually don't. And so we talk to each other, write and wire each other, call each other short and long distance across land and sea, clasp hands with each other at meeting and at parting, fight each other and even destroy each other because of this always somewhat thwarted effort to break through walls to each other. As a character in a play once said, "We're all of us sentenced to solitary confinement inside our own skins."

Personal lyricism is the outcry of prisoner to prisoner from the cell in solitary where each is confined for the duration of his life.

I once saw a group of little girls on a Mississippi sidewalk, all dolled up in their mothers' and sisters' castoff finery, old raggedy ball gowns and plumed hats and high-heeled slippers, enacting a meeting of ladies in a parlor with a perfect mimicry of polite Southern gush and simper. But one child was not satisfied with the attention paid her enraptured performance by the others, they were too involved in their own performances to suit her, so she stretched out her skinny arms and threw back her skinny neck and shrieked to the deaf heavens and her equally oblivious playmates, "Look at me, look at me, look at me!"

And then her mother's high-heeled slippers threw her off balance and she fell to the sidewalk in a great howling tangle of soiled white satin and torn pink net, and still nobody looked at her.

I wonder if she is not, now, a Southern writer.

Of course it is not only Southern writers, of lyrical bent, who engage in such histrionics and shout, "Look at me!" Perhaps it is a parable of all artists. And not always do we topple over and land in a tangle of trappings that don't fit us. However, it is well to be aware of that peril, and not to content yourself with a demand for attention, to know that out of your personal lyricism, your sidewalk histrionics, something has to be created that will not only attract observers but participants in the performance.

I try very hard to do that.

The fact that I want you to observe what I do for your possible pleasure and to give you knowledge of things that I feel I may know better than you, because my world is different from yours, as different as every man's world is from the world of others, is not enough excuse for a personal lyricism that has not yet mastered its necessary trick of rising above the singular to the plural concern, from personal to general import. But for years and years now, which may have passed like a dream because of this obsession, I have been trying to learn how to perform this trick and make it truthful, and sometimes I feel that I am able to do it. Sometimes, when the enraptured street-corner performer in me cries out "Look at me!," I feel that my hazardous footwear and fantastic regalia may not quite throw me off balance. Then, suddenly, you fellow-performers in the sidewalk show may turn to give me your attention and allow me to hold it, at least for the interval between 8:40 and 11 something P.M.

Eleven years ago this month of March, when I was far closer than I knew, only nine months away from that long-delayed, but always expected, something that I lived for, the time when I would first catch and hold an audience's attention, I wrote my first preface to a long play. The final paragraph went like this:

"There is too much to say and not enough time to say it. Nor is there power enough. I am not a good writer. Sometimes I am a very bad writer indeed. There is hardly a successful writer in the field who cannot write circles around me . . . but I think of writing as something more organic than words, something closer to being and action. I want to work more and more with a more plastic theatre than the one I have (worked with) before. I have never for one moment doubted that there are people—millions!—to say things to. We come to each other, gradually, but with love. It is the short reach of my arms that hinders, not the length and multiplicity of theirs. With love and with honesty, the embrace is inevitable."

This characteristically emotional, if not rhetorical, statement of mine at that time seems to suggest that I thought of myself as having a highly personal, even intimate relationship with people who go to see plays. I did and I still do. A morbid shyness once prevented me from having much direct communication with people, and possibly that is why I began to write to them plays and stories. But even now when that tongue-locking, face-flushing, silent and crouching timidity has worn off with the passage of the troublesome youth that it sprang from, I still find it somehow easier to "level with" crowds of strangers in the hushed twilight of orchestra and balcony sections of theatres than with individuals across a table from me. Their being strangers somehow makes them more familiar and more approachable, easier to talk to.

Of course I know that I have sometimes presumed too much upon corresponding sympathies and interest in those to whom I talk boldly, and this has led to rejections that were painful and costly enough to inspire more prudence. But when I weigh one thing against another, an easy liking against a hard respect, the balance always tips the same way, and whatever the risk of being turned a cold shoulder, I still don't want to talk to people only about the surface aspects of their lives, the sort of things that acquaintances laugh and chatter about on ordinary social occasions.

I feel that they get plenty of that, and heaven knows so do I, before and after the little interval of time in which I have their attention and say what I have to say to them. The discretion of social conversation, even among friends, is exceeded only by the discretion of "the deep six," that grave wherein nothing is mentioned at all. Emily Dickinson, that lyrical spinster of Amherst, Massachusetts, who wore a strict and savage heart on a taffeta sleeve, commented wryly on that kind of posthumous discourse among friends in these lines:

> *I died for beauty, but was scarce*
> *Adjusted in the tomb,*
> *When one who died for truth was lain*
> *In an adjoining room.*
>
> *He questioned softly why I failed?*
> *"For beauty," I replied.*
> *"And I for truth,—the two are one;*
> *We brethren are," he said.*

And so, as kinsmen met a night,
We talked between the rooms,
Until the moss had reached our lips,
And covered up our names.

Meanwhile!—I want to go on talking to you as freely and intimately about what we live and die for as if I knew you better than anyone else whom you know.

—Tennessee Williams

CAT ON A
HOT TIN ROOF

CHARACTERS OF THE PLAY

MARGARET
BRICK
MAE, sometimes called Sister Woman
BIG MAMA
DIXIE, a little girl
BIG DADDY
REVEREND TOOKER
GOOPER, sometimes called Brother Man
DOCTOR BAUGH, pronounced "Baw"
LACEY, a Negro servant
SOOKEY, another
Another little girl and two small boys

(The playing script of Act III also includes TRIXIE, another little girl, also DAISY, BRIGHTIE and SMALL, servants.)

Cat on a Hot Tin Roof was presented at the Morosco Theatre in New York on March 24, 1955, by The Playwrights' Company. It was directed by Elia Kazan, with the following cast:

LACEY	MAXWELL GLANVILLE
SOOKEY	MUSA WILLIAMS
MARGARET	BARBARA BEL GEDDES
BRICK	BEN GAZZARA
MAE	MADELEINE SHERWOOD
GOOPER	PAT HINGLE
BIG MAMA	MILDRED DUNNOCK
DIXIE	PAULINE HAHN
BUSTER	DARRYL RICHARD
SONNY	SETH EDWARDS
TRIXIE	JANICE DUNN
BIG DADDY	BURL IVES
REVEREND TOOKER	FRED STEWART
DOCTOR BAUGH	R. G. ARMSTRONG
DAISY	EVA VAUGHAN SMITH
BRIGHTIE	BROWNIE MCGHEE
SMALL	SONNY TERRY

Leading Members of the cast of the Avon Production released by M-G-M

MARGARET POLLITT	ELIZABETH TAYLOR
BRICK POLLITT	PAUL NEWMAN
POLLITT, SR. (BIG DADDY)	BURL IVES
GOOPER POLLITT	JACK CARSON
BIG MAMA	JUDITH ANDERSON
MAE POLLITT	MADELEINE SHERWOOD

Directed by RICHARD BROOKS

Produced by LAWRENCE WEINGARTEN

Screenplay by RICHARD BROOKS

NOTES FOR THE DESIGNER

The set is the bed-sitting-room of a plantation home in the Mississippi Delta. It is along an upstairs gallery which probably runs around the entire house; it has two pairs of very wide doors opening onto the gallery; showing white balustrades against a fair summer sky that fades into dusk and night during the course of the play, which occupies precisely the time of its performance, excepting, of course, the fifteen minutes of intermission.

Perhaps the style of the room is not what you would expect in the home of the Delta's biggest cotton-planter. It is Victorian with a touch of the Far East. It hasn't changed much since it was occupied by the original owners of the place, Jack Straw and Peter Ochello, a pair of old bachelors who shared this room all their lives together. In other words, the room must evoke some ghosts; it is gently and poetically haunted by a relationship that must have involved a tenderness which was uncommon. This may be irrelevant or unnecessary, but I once saw a reproduction of a faded photograph of the verandah of Robert Louis Stevenson's home on that Samoan Island where he spent his last years, and there was a quality of tender light on weathered wood, such as porch furniture made of bamboo and wicker, exposed to tropical suns and tropical rains, which came to mind when I thought about the set for this play, bringing also to mind the grace and comfort of light, the reassurance it gives, on a late and fair afternoon in summer, the way that no matter what, even dread of death, is gently touched and soothed by it. For the set is the background for a play that deals with human extremities of emotion, and it needs that softness behind it.

The bathroom door, showing only pale-blue tile and silver towel racks, is in one side wall; the hall door in the opposite wall. Two articles of furniture need mention: a big double bed which staging should make a functional part of the set as often as suitable, the surface of which should be slightly raked to make figures on it seen more easily; and against the wall space between the two huge double doors upstage: a monumental monstrosity peculiar to our times, a *huge* console combination of radio-phonograph (Hi-Fi with three speakers), TV set *and* liquor cabinet, bearing and containing many glasses and bottles, all in one piece, which is a composition of muted silver tones, and the opalescent tones of reflecting glass, a chromatic link, this thing, between the sepia (tawny gold) tones of the interior and the cool (white and blue) tones of the gallery and sky. This piece of furniture (?!), this monument, is a very complete and compact little shrine to virtually all the comforts and illusions behind which we hide from such things as the characters in the play are faced with. . . . The set should be far less realistic than I have so far implied in this description of it. I think the walls below the ceiling should dissolve mysteriously into air; the set should be roofed by the sky; stars and moon suggested by traces of milky pallor, as if they were observed through a telescope lens out of focus.

Anything else I can think of? Oh, yes, fanlights (transoms shaped like an open glass fan) above all the doors in the set, with panes of blue and amber, and above all, the designer should take as many pains to give the actors room to move about freely (to show their restlessness, their passion for breaking out) as if it were a set for a ballet.

An evening in summer. The action is continuous, with two intermissions.

ACT ONE

At the rise of the curtain someone is taking a shower in the bathroom, the door of which is half open. A pretty young woman, with anxious lines in her face, enters the bedroom and crosses to the bathroom door.

MARGARET [*shouting above roar of water*]:
One of those no-neck monsters hit me with a hot buttered biscuit so I have t' change!

> [*Margaret's voice is both rapid and drawling. In her long speeches she has the vocal tricks of a priest delivering a liturgical chant, the lines are almost sung, always continuing a little beyond her breath so she has to gasp for another. Sometimes she intersperses the lines with a little wordless singing, such as "Da-da-daaaa!"*]
>
> [*Water turns off and Brick calls out to her, but is still unseen. A tone of politely feigned interest, masking indifference, or worse, is characteristic of his speech with Margaret.*]

BRICK:
Wha'd you say, Maggie? Water was on s' loud I couldn't hearya. . . .

MARGARET:
Well, I!—just remarked that!—one of th' no-neck monsters messed up m' lovely lace dress so I got t'—cha-a-ange. . . .

> [*She opens and kicks shut drawers of the dresser.*]

BRICK:
Why d'ya call Gooper's kiddies no-neck monsters?

MARGARET:
Because they've got no necks! Isn't that a good enough reason?

BRICK:
Don't they have any necks?

MARGARET:
None visible. Their fat little heads are set on their fat little bodies without a bit of connection.

BRICK:
That's too bad.

MARGARET:
Yes, it's too bad because you can't wring their necks if they've got no necks to wring! Isn't that right, honey?

> [*She steps out of her dress, stands in a slip of ivory satin and lace.*]

Yep, they're no-neck monsters, all no-neck people are monsters . . .

> [*Children shriek downstairs.*]

Hear them? Hear them screaming? I don't know where their voice-boxes are located since they don't have necks. I tell you I got so nervous at that table tonight I thought I would throw back my head and utter a scream you could hear across the Arkansas border an' parts of Louisiana an' Tennessee. I said to your charming sister-in-law, Mae, honey, couldn't you feed those precious little things at a separate table with an oilcloth cover? They make such a mess an' the lace cloth looks *so* pretty! She made enormous eyes at me and said, "Ohhh, noooooo! On Big Daddy's birthday? Why, he would never forgive me!" Well, I want you to know, Big Daddy hadn't been at the table two minutes with those five no-neck monsters slobbering and drooling over their food before he threw down his fork an' shouted, "Fo' God's sake, Gooper, why don't you put them pigs at a trough in th' kitchen?"—Well, I swear, I simply could have di-ied!

Think of it, Brick, they've got five of them and number six is coming. They've brought the whole bunch down

here like animals to display at a county fair. Why, they
have those children doin' tricks all the time! "Junior,
show Big Daddy how you do this, show Big Daddy how
you do that, say your little piece fo' Big Daddy, Sister.
Show your dimples, Sugar. Brother, show Big Daddy
how you stand on your head!"—It goes on all the time,
along with constant little remarks and innuendos about
the fact that you and I have not produced any children,
are totally childless and therefore totally useless!—Of
course it's comical but it's also disgusting since it's so
obvious what they're up to!

BRICK [*without interest*]:
What are they up to, Maggie?

MARGARET:
Why, you know what they're up to!

BRICK [*appearing*]:
No, I don't know what they're up to.

[*He stands there in the bathroom doorway drying his
hair with a towel and hanging on to the towel rack
because one ankle is broken, plastered and bound.
He is still slim and firm as a boy. His liquor hasn't
started tearing him down outside. He has the addi-
tional charm of that cool air of detachment that people have who have given up the struggle. But now
and then, when disturbed, something flashes behind
it, like lightning in a fair sky, which shows that at
some deeper level he is far from peaceful. Perhaps
in a stronger light he would show some signs of deli-
quescence, but the fading, still warm, light from the
gallery treats him gently.*]

MARGARET:
I'll tell you what they're up to, boy of mine!—They're
up to cutting you out of your father's estate, and—

[*She freezes momentarily before her next remark.
Her voice drops as if it were somehow a personally
embarrassing admission.*]

—Now we know that Big Daddy's dyin' of—*cancer*. . . .

[*There are voices on the lawn below: long-drawn calls across distance. Margaret raises her lovely bare arms and powders her armpits with a light sigh.*

[*She adjusts the angle of a magnifying mirror to straighten an eyelash, then rises fretfully saying:*]

There's so much light in the room it—

BRICK [*softly but sharply*]:
Do we?

MARGARET:
Do we what?

BRICK:
Know Big Daddy's dyin' of cancer?

MARGARET:
Got the report today.

BRICK:
Oh . . .

MARGARET [*letting down bamboo blinds which cast long, gold-fretted shadows over the room*]:
Yep, got th' report just now . . . it didn't surprise me, Baby. . . .

[*Her voice has range, and music; sometimes it drops low as a boy's and you have a sudden image of her playing boys' games as a child.*]

I recognized the symptoms soon's we got here last spring and I'm willin' to bet you that Brother Man and his wife were pretty sure of it, too. That more than likely explains why their usual summer migration to the coolness of the Great Smokies was passed up this summer in favor of—hustlin' down here ev'ry whipstitch with their whole screamin' tribe! And why so many allusions have been made to Rainbow Hill lately. You know what Rainbow Hill is? Place that's famous for treatin' alcoholics an' dope fiends in the movies!

BRICK:
I'm not in the movies.

MARGARET:
No, and you don't take dope. Otherwise you're a perfect
candidate for Rainbow Hill, Baby, and that's where they
aim to ship you—over my dead body! Yep, over my
dead body they'll ship you there, but nothing would
please them better. Then Brother Man could get a-hold
of the purse strings and dole out remittances to us,
maybe get power-of-attorney and sign checks for us and
cut off our credit wherever, whenever he wanted! Son-
of-a-bitch!—How'd you like that, Baby?—Well, you've
been doin' just about ev'rything in your power to bring
it about, you've just been doin' ev'rything you can think
of to aid and abet them in this scheme of theirs! Quittin'
work, devoting yourself to the occupation of drinkin'!—
Breakin' your ankle last night on the high school athletic
field: doin' what? Jumpin' hurdles? At two or three in
the morning? Just fantastic! Got in the paper. *Clarksdale
Register* carried a nice little item about it, human interest
story about a well-known former athlete stagin' a one-
man track meet on the Glorious Hill High School athletic field last night, but was slightly out of condition and
didn't clear the first hurdle! Brother Man Gooper claims
he exercised his influence t' keep it from goin' out over
AP or UP or every goddam "P."
But, Brick? You still have one big advantage!

[*During the above swift flood of words, Brick has
reclined with contrapuntal leisure on the snowy surface of the bed and has rolled over carefully on his
side or belly.*]

BRICK [*wryly*]:
Did you *say* something, Maggie?

MARGARET:
Big Daddy dotes on you, honey. And he can't stand
Brother Man and Brother Man's wife, that monster of
fertility, Mae; she's downright odious to him! Know how
I know? By little expressions that flicker over his face
when that woman is holding fo'th on one of her choice
topics such as—how she refused twilight sleep!—when
the twins were delivered! Because she feels mother-

hood's an experience that a woman ought to experience fully!—in order to fully appreciate the wonder and beauty of it! HAH!

[*This loud "HAH!" is accompanied by a violent action such as slamming a drawer shut.*]

—and how she made Brother Man come in an' stand beside her in the delivery room so he would not miss out on the "wonder and beauty" of it either!—producin' those no-neck monsters. . . .

[*A speech of this kind would be antipathetic from almost anybody but Margaret; she makes it oddly funny, because her eyes constantly twinkle and her voice shakes with laughter which is basically indulgent.*]

—Big Daddy shares my attitude toward those two! As for me, well—I give him a laugh now and then and he tolerates me. In fact!—I sometimes suspect that Big Daddy harbors a little unconscious "lech" fo' me. . . .

BRICK:
What makes you think that Big Daddy has a lech for you, Maggie?

MARGARET:
Way he always drops his eyes down my body when I'm talkin' to him, drops his eyes to my boobs an' licks his old chops! Ha ha!

BRICK:
That kind of talk is disgusting.

MARGARET:
Did anyone ever tell you that you're an ass-aching Puritan, Brick?
I think it's mighty fine that that ole fellow, on the doorstep of death, still takes in my shape with what I think is deserved appreciation!
And you wanta know something else? Big Daddy didn't know how many little Maes and Goopers had been produced! "How many kids have you got?" he asked at the table, just like Brother Man and his wife were new acquaintances to him! Big Mama said he was jokin', but that ole boy wasn't jokin', Lord, no!

And when they infawmed him that they had five already
and were turning out number six!—the news seemed to
come as a sort of unpleasant surprise . . .

[*Children yell below.*]

Scream, monsters!

[*Turns to Brick with a sudden, gay, charming smile
which fades as she notices that he is not looking at
her but into fading gold space· with a troubled
expression.*

[*It is constant rejection that makes her humor
"bitchy."*]

Yes, you should of been at that supper-table, Baby.

[*Whenever she calls him "baby" the word is a soft
caress.*]

Y'know, Big Daddy, bless his ole sweet soul, he's the
dearest ole thing in the world, but he does hunch over
his food as if he preferred not to notice anything else.
Well, Mae an' Gooper were side by side at the table,
direckly across from Big Daddy, watchin' his face like
hawks while they jawed an' jabbered about the cuteness
an' brillance of th' no-neck monsters!

[*She giggles with a hand fluttering at her throat and
her breast and her long throat arched.*

[*She comes downstage and re-creates the scene with
voice and gesture.*]

And the no-neck monsters were ranged around the
table, some in high chairs and some on th' *Books of
Knowledge,* all in fancy little paper caps in honor of Big
Daddy's birthday, and all through dinner, well, I want
you to know that Brother Man an' his partner never
once, for one moment, stopped exchanging pokes an'
pinches an' kicks an' signs an' signals!—Why, they were
like a couple of cardsharps fleecing a sucker.—Even Big
Mama, bless her ole sweet soul, she isn't th' quickest an'
brightest thing in the world, she finally noticed, at last,
an' said to Gooper, "Gooper, what are you an' Mae
makin' all these signs at each other about?"—I swear t'
goodness, I nearly choked on my chicken!

[*Margaret, back at the dressing-table, still doesn't see*

> *Brick. He is watching her with a look that is not quite definable.—Amused? shocked? contemptuous?—part of those and part of something else.*]

Y'know—your brother Gooper still cherishes the illusion he took a giant step up on the social ladder when he married Miss Mae Flynn of the Memphis Flynns.

> [*Margaret moves about the room as she talks, stops before the mirror, moves on.*]

But I have a piece of Spanish news for Gooper. The Flynns never had a thing in this world but money and they lost that, they were nothing at all but fairly successful climbers. Of course, Mae Flynn came out in Memphis eight years before I made my debut in Nashville, but I had friends at Ward-Belmont who came from Memphis and they used to come to see me and I used to go to see them for Christmas and spring vacations, and so I know who rates an' who doesn't rate in Memphis society. Why, y'know ole Papa Flynn, he barely escaped doing time in the Federal pen for shady manipulations on th' stock market when his chain stores crashed, and as for Mae having been a cotton carnival queen, as they remind us so often, lest we forget, well, that's one honor that I don't envy her for!—Sit on a brass throne on a tacky float an' ride down Main Street, smilin', bowin', and blowin' kisses to all the trash on the street—

> [*She picks out a pair of jeweled sandals and rushes to the dressing-table.*]

Why, year before last, when Susan McPheeters was singled out fo' that honor, y'know what happened to her? Y'know what happened to poor little Susie McPheeters?

BRICK [*absently*]:
No. What happened to little Susie McPheeters?

MARGARET:
Somebody spit tobacco juice in her face.

BRICK [*dreamily*]:
Somebody spit tobacco juice in her face?

MARGARET:
That's right, some old drunk leaned out of a window in

the Hotel Gayoso and yelled, "Hey, Queen, hey, hey, there, Queenie!" Poor Susie looked up and flashed him a radiant smile and he shot out a squirt of tobacco juice right in poor Susie's face.

BRICK:
Well, what d'you know about that.

MARGARET [*gaily*]:
What do I know about it? I was there, I saw it!

BRICK [*absently*]:
Must have been kind of funny.

MARGARET:
Susie didn't think so. Had hysterics. Screamed like a banshee. They had to stop th' parade an' remove her from her throne an' go on with—

   [*She catches sight of him in the mirror, gasps slightly, wheels about to face him. Count ten.*]
—Why are you looking at me like that?

BRICK [*whistling softly, now*]:
Like what, Maggie?

MARGARET [*intensely, fearfully*]:
The way y' were lookin' at me just now, befo' I caught your eye in the mirror and you started t' whistle! I don't know how t' describe it but it froze my blood!—I've caught you lookin' at me like that so often lately. What are you thinkin' of when you look at me like that?

BRICK:
I wasn't conscious of lookin' at you, Maggie.

MARGARET:
Well, I was conscious of it! What were you thinkin'?

BRICK:
I don't remember thinking of anything, Maggie.

MARGARET:
Don't you think I know that—? Don't you—?—Think I know that—?

BRICK [*coolly*]:
Know *what*, Maggie?

MARGARET [*struggling for expression*]:
That I've gone through this—*hideous!*—*transformation*, become—*hard! Frantic!*

[*Then she adds, almost tenderly:*]
—*cruel!!*
That's what you've been observing in me lately. How could y' help but observe it? That's all right. I'm not—thin-skinned anymore, can't afford t' be thin-skinned anymore.

[*She is now recovering her power.*]
—But Brick? Brick?

BRICK:
Did you say something?

MARGARET:
I was *goin'* t' say something: that I get—lonely. Very!

BRICK:
Ev'rybody gets that . . .

MARGARET:
Living with someone you love can be lonelier—than living entirely *alone!*—if the one that y' love doesn't love you. . . .

[*There is a pause. Brick hobbles downstage and asks, without looking at her:*]

BRICK:
Would you like to live alone, Maggie?

[*Another pause: then—after she has caught a quick, hurt breath:*]

MARGARET:
No!—God!—I wouldn't!

[*Another gasping breath. She forcibly controls what must have been an impulse to cry out. We see her deliberately, very forcibly, going all the way back to the world in which you can talk about ordinary matters.*]

Did you have a nice shower?

BRICK:
Uh-huh.

MARGARET:
Was the water cool?

BRICK:
No.

MARGARET:
But it made y' feel fresh, huh?

BRICK:
Fresher. . . .

MARGARET:
I know something would make y' feel *much* fresher!

BRICK:
What?

MARGARET:
An alcohol rub. Or cologne, a rub with cologne!

BRICK:
That's good after a workout but I haven't been workin'
out, Maggie.

MARGARET:
You've kept in good shape, though.

BRICK [*indifferently*]:
You think so, Maggie?

MARGARET:
I always thought drinkin' men lost their looks, but I was
plainly mistaken.

BRICK [*wryly*]:
Why, thanks, Maggie.

MARGARET:
You're the only drinkin' man I know that it never seems
t' put fat on.

BRICK:
I'm gettin' softer, Maggie.

MARGARET:
Well, sooner or later it's bound to soften you up. It was
just beginning to soften up Skipper when—

[*She stops short.*]

I'm sorry. I never could keep my fingers off a sore—I
wish you *would* lose your looks. If you did it would
make the martyrdom of Saint Maggie a little more bear-
able. But no such goddam luck. I actually believe you've
gotten better looking since you've gone on the bottle.
Yeah, a person who didn't know you would think you'd
never had a tense nerve in your body or a strained
muscle.

[*There are sounds of croquet on the lawn below: the
click of mallets, light voices, near and distant.*]

Of course, you always had that detached quality as if
you were playing a game without much concern over
whether you won or lost, and now that you've lost the
game, not lost but just quit playing, you have that rare
sort of charm that usually only happens in very old or
hopelessly sick people, the charm of the defeated.—You
look so cool, so cool, so enviably cool.

[*Music is heard.*]

They're playing croquet. The moon has appeared and
it's white, just beginning to turn a little bit yellow. . . .
You were a wonderful lover. . . .
Such a wonderful person to go to bed with, and I think
mostly because you were really indifferent to it. Isn't
that right? Never had any anxiety about it, did it natu-
rally, easily, slowly, with absolute confidence and perfect
calm, more like opening a door for a lady or seating her
at a table than giving expression to any longing for her.
Your indifference made you wonderful at lovemaking—
strange?—but true. . . .
You know, if I thought you would never, never, *never*
make love to me again—I would go downstairs to the
kitchen and pick out the longest and sharpest knife I

could find and stick it straight into my heart, I swear that I would!
But one thing I don't have is the charm of the defeated, my hat is still in the ring, and I am determined to win!

[*There is the sound of croquet mallets hitting croquet balls.*]

—What is the victory of a cat on a hot tin roof?—I wish I knew. . . .
Just staying on it, I guess, as long as she can. . . .

[*More croquet sounds.*]

Later tonight I'm going to tell you I love you an' maybe by that time you'll be drunk enough to believe me. Yes, they're playing croquet. . . .
Big Daddy is dying of cancer. . . .
What were you thinking of when I caught you looking at me like that? Were you thinking of Skipper?

[*Brick takes up his crutch, rises.*]

Oh, excuse me, forgive me, but laws of silence don't work! No, laws of silence don't work. . . .

[*Brick crosses to the bar, takes a quick drink, and rubs his head with a towel.*]

Laws of silence don't work. . . .
When something is festering in your memory or your imagination, laws of silence don't work, it's just like shutting a door and locking it on a house on fire in hope of forgetting that the house is burning. But not facing a fire doesn't put it out. Silence about a thing just magnifies it. It grows and festers in silence, becomes malignant. . . .
Get dressed, Brick.

[*He drops his crutch.*]

BRICK:
I've dropped my crutch.

[*He has stopped rubbing his hair dry but still stands hanging on to the towel rack in a white towel-cloth robe.*]

MARGARET:
Lean on me.

BRICK:
No, just give me my crutch.

MARGARET:
Lean on my shoulder.

BRICK:
I don't want to lean on your shoulder, I want my crutch!

[*This is spoken like sudden lightning.*]

Are you going to give me my crutch or do I have to get
down on my knees on the floor and—

MARGARET:
Here, here, take it, take it!

[*She has thrust the crutch at him.*]

BRICK [*hobbling out*]:
Thanks . . .

MARGARET:
We mustn't scream at each other, the walls in this house
have ears. . . .

[*He hobbles directly to liquor cabinet to get a new
drink.*]

—but that's the first time I've heard you raise your voice
in a long time, Brick. A crack in the wall?—Of
composure?
—I think that's a good sign. . . .
A sign of nerves in a player on the defensive!

[*Brick turns and smiles at her coolly over his fresh
drink.*]

BRICK:
It just hasn't happened yet, Maggie.

MARGARET:
What?

BRICK:
The click I get in my head when I've had enough of this
stuff to make me peaceful. . . .
Will you do me a favor?

MARGARET:
Maybe I will. What favor?

BRICK:
Just, just keep your voice down!

MARGARET [*in a hoarse whisper*]:
I'll do you that favor, I'll speak in a whisper, if not shut up completely, if *you* will do *me* a favor and make that drink your last one till after the party.

BRICK:
What party?

MARGARET:
Big Daddy's birthday party.

BRICK:
Is this Big Daddy's birthday?

MARGARET:
You know this is Big Daddy's birthday!

BRICK:
No, I don't, I forgot it.

MARGARET:
Well, I remembered it for you. . . .
> [*They are both speaking as breathlessly as a pair of kids after a fight, drawing deep exhausted breaths and looking at each other with faraway eyes, shaking and panting together as if they had broken apart from a violent struggle.*]

BRICK:
Good for you, Maggie.

MARGARET:
You just have to scribble a few lines on this card.

BRICK:
You scribble something, Maggie.

MARGARET:
It's got to be your handwriting; it's your present, I've given him my present; it's got to be your handwriting!

[*The tension between them is building again, the voices becoming shrill once more.*]

BRICK:
I didn't get him a present.

MARGARET:
I got one for you.

BRICK:
All right. You write the card, then.

MARGARET:
And have him know you didn't remember his birthday?

BRICK:
I didn't remember his birthday.

MARGARET:
You don't have to prove you didn't!

BRICK:
I don't want to fool him about it.

MARGARET:
Just write "Love, Brick!" for God's—

BRICK:
No.

MARGARET:
You've *got* to!

BRICK:
I don't have to do anything I don't want to do. You keep forgetting the conditions on which I agreed to stay on living with you.

MARGARET [*out before she knows it*]:
I'm not living with you. We occupy the same cage.

BRICK:
You've got to remember the conditions agreed on.

MARGARET:
They're impossible conditions!

BRICK:
Then why don't you—?

MARGARET:
HUSH! Who is out there? Is somebody at the door?
   [*There are footsteps in hall.*]

MAE [*outside*]:
May I enter a moment?

MARGARET:
Oh, *you!* Sure. Come in, Mae.
   [*Mae enters bearing aloft the bow of a young lady's archery set.*]

MAE:
Brick, is this thing yours?

MARGARET:
Why, Sister Woman—that's my Diana Trophy. Won it at the intercollegiate archery contest on the Ole Miss campus.

MAE:
It's a mighty dangerous thing to leave exposed round a house full of nawmal rid-blooded children attracted t'weapons.

MARGARET:
"Nawmal rid-blooded children attracted t'weapons" ought t'be taught to keep their hands off things that don't belong to them.

MAE:
Maggie, honey, if you had children of your own you'd know how funny that is. Will you please lock this up and put the key out of reach?

MARGARET:
Sister Woman, nobody is plotting the destruction of your kiddies.—Brick and I still have our special archers' license. We're goin' deer-huntin' on Moon Lake as soon as the season starts. I love to run with dogs through chilly woods, run, run, leap over obstructions—
   [*She goes into the closet carrying the bow.*]

MAE:
How's the injured ankle, Brick?

BRICK:
Doesn't hurt. Just itches.

MAE:
Oh, my! Brick—Brick, you should've been downstairs after supper! Kiddies put on a show. Polly played the piano, Buster an' Sonny drums, an' then they turned out the lights an' Dixie an' Trixie puhfawmed a toe dance in fairy costume with *spahkluhs!* Big Daddy just beamed! He just beamed!

MARGARET [*from the closet with a sharp laugh*]:
Oh, I bet. It breaks my heart that we missed it!
      [*She reenters.*]
But Mae? Why did y'give dawgs' names to all your kiddies?

MAE:
Dogs' names?

      [*Margaret has made this observation as she goes to raise the bamboo blinds, since the sunset glare has diminished. In crossing she winks at Brick.*]

MARGARET [*sweetly*]:
Dixie, Trixie, Buster, Sonny, Polly!—Sounds like four dogs and a parrot . . . animal act in a circus!

MAE:
Maggie?
      [*Margaret turns with a smile.*]
Why are you so catty?

MARGARET:
Cause I'm a cat! But why can't *you* take a joke, Sister Woman?

MAE:
Nothin' pleases me more than a joke that's funny. You know the real names of our kiddies. Buster's real name is Robert. Sonny's real name is Saunders. Trixie's real name is Marlene and Dixie's—

[*Someone downstairs calls for her. "Hey, Mae!"—She rushes to door, saying:*]

Intermission is over!

MARGARET [*as Mae closes door*]:
I wonder what Dixie's real name is?

BRICK:
Maggie, being catty doesn't help things any . . .

MARGARET:
I know! *WHY!*—Am I so catty?—Cause I'm consumed with envy an' eaten up with longing?—Brick, I've laid out your beautiful Shantung silk suit from Rome and one of your monogrammed silk shirts. I'll put your cuff-links in it, those lovely star sapphires I get you to wear so rarely. . . .

BRICK:
I can't get trousers on over this plaster cast.

MARGARET:
Yes, you can, I'll help you.

BRICK:
I'm not going to get dressed, Maggie.

MARGARET:
Will you just put on a pair of white silk pajamas?

BRICK:
Yes, I'll do that, Maggie.

MARGARET:
Thank you, thank you so *much!*

BRICK:
Don't mention it.

MARGARET:
Oh, Brick! How long does it have t' go on? This punishment? Haven't I done time enough, haven't I served my term, can't I apply for a—pardon?

BRICK:
Maggie, you're spoiling my liquor. Lately your voice al-

ways sounds like you'd been running upstairs to warn
somebody that the house was on fire!

MARGARET:
Well, no wonder, no wonder. Y'know what I feel like,
Brick?

> [*Children's and grownups' voices are blended, below,
> in a loud but uncertain rendition of "My Wild Irish
> Rose."*]

I feel all the time like a cat on a hot tin roof!

BRICK:
Then jump off the roof, jump off it, cats can jump off
roofs and land on their four feet uninjured!

MARGARET:
Oh, yes!

BRICK:
Do it!—fo' God's sake, do it . . .

MARGARET:
Do what?

BRICK:
Take a lover!

MARGARET:
I can't see a man but you! Even with my eyes closed, I
just see you! Why don't you get ugly, Brick, why don't
you please get fat or ugly or something so I could
stand it?

> [*She rushes to hall door, opens it, listens.*]

The concert is still going on! Bravo, no-necks, bravo!

> [*She slams and locks door fiercely.*]

BRICK:
What did you lock the door for?

MARGARET:
To give us a little privacy for a while.

BRICK:
You know better, Maggie.

MARGARET:
No, I don't know better. . . .

> [*She rushes to gallery doors, draws the rose-silk drapes across them.*]

BRICK:
Don't make a fool of yourself.

MARGARET:
I don't mind makin' a fool of myself over you!

BRICK:
I mind, Maggie. I feel embarrassed for you.

MARGARET:
Feel embarrassed! But don't continue my torture. I can't live on and on under these circumstances.

BRICK:
You agreed to—

MARGARET:
I know but—

BRICK:
—Accept that condition!

MARGARET:
I CAN'T! CAN'T! CAN'T!

> [*She seizes his shoulder.*]

BRICK:
Let go!

> [*He breaks away from her and seizes the small boudoir chair and raises it like a lion-tamer facing a big circus cat.*
> [*Count five. She stares at him with her fist pressed to her mouth, then bursts into shrill, almost hysterical laughter. He remains grave for a moment, then grins and puts the chair down.*
> [*Big Mama calls through closed door.*]

BIG MAMA:
Son? Son? Son?

BRICK:
What is it, Big Mama?

BIG MAMA [*outside*]:
Oh, son! We got the most wonderful news about Big
Daddy. I just had t' run up an' tell you right this—

[*She rattles the knob.*]

—What's this door doin', locked, faw? You all think
there's robbers in the house?

MARGARET:
Big Mama, Brick is dressin', he's not dressed yet.

BIG MAMA:
That's all right, it won't be the first time I've seen Brick
not dressed. Come on, open this door!

[*Margaret, with a grimace, goes to unlock and open
the hall door, as Brick hobbles rapidly to the bathroom and kicks the door shut. Big Mama has disap-
peared from the hall.*]

MARGARET:
Big Mama?

[*Big Mama appears through the opposite gallery
doors behind Margaret, huffing and puffing like an
old bulldog. She is a short, stout woman; her sixty
years and 170 pounds have left her somewhat breathless most of the time; she's always tensed like a boxer,
or rather, a Japanese wrestler. Her "family" was
maybe a little superior to Big Daddy's, but not much.
She wears a black or silver lace dress and at least
half a million in flashy gems. She is very sincere.*]

BIG MAMA [*loudly, startling Margaret*]:
Here—I come through Gooper's and Mae's gall'ry door.
Where's Brick? *Brick*—Hurry on out of there, son, I just
have a second and want to give you the news about Big
Daddy.—I hate locked doors in a house. . . .

MARGARET [*with affected lightness*]:
I've noticed you do, Big Mama, but people have got to
have *some* moments of privacy, don't they?

BIG MAMA:

No, ma'am, not in *my* house. [*Without pause*] Whacha took off you' dress faw? I thought that little lace dress was so sweet on yuh, honey.

MARGARET:

I thought it looked sweet on me, too, but one of m' cute little table-partners used it for a napkin so—!

BIG MAMA [*picking up stockings on floor*]:
What?

MARGARET:

You know, Big Mama, Mae and Gooper's so touchy about those children—thanks, Big Mama . . .

   [*Big Mama has thrust the picked-up stockings in Margaret's hand with a grunt.*]

—that you just don't dare to suggest there's any room for improvement in their—

BIG MAMA:

Brick, hurry out!—Shoot, Maggie, you just don't like children.

MARGARET:

I do SO like children! Adore them!—well brought up!

BIG MAMA [*gentle—loving*]:
Well, why don't you have some and bring them up well, then, instead of all the time pickin' on Gooper's an' Mae's?

GOOPER [*shouting up the stairs*]:
Hey, hey, Big Mama, Betsy an' Hugh got to go, waitin' t' tell yuh g'by!

BIG MAMA:

Tell 'em to hold their hawses, I'll be right down in a jiffy!

   [*She turns to the bathroom door and calls out.*]

Son? Can you hear me in there?

   [*There is a muffled answer.*]

We just got the full report from the laboratory at the

Ochsner Clinic, completely negative, son, ev'rything negative, right on down the line! Nothin' a-tall's wrong with
him but some little functional thing called a spastic
colon. Can you hear me, son?

MARGARET:
He can hear you, Big Mama.

BIG MAMA:
Then why don't he say something? God Almighty, a
piece of news like that should make him shout. It made
me shout, I can tell you. I shouted and sobbed and fell
right down on my knees—Look!

   [*She pulls up her skirt.*]

See the bruises where I hit my kneecaps? Took both
doctors to haul me back on my feet!

   [*She laughs—she always laughs like hell at herself.*]

Big Daddy was furious with me! But ain't that wonderful news?

   [*Facing bathroom again, she continues:*]

After all the anxiety we been through to git a report
like that on Big Daddy's birthday? Big Daddy tried to
hide how much of a load that news took off his mind,
but didn't fool *me*. He was mighty close to crying about
it *himself!*

   [*Goodbyes are shouted downstairs, and she rushes
   to door.*]

Hold those people down there, don't let them go!—Now,
git dressed, we're all comin' up to this room fo' Big
Daddy's birthday party because of your ankle.—How's
his ankle, Maggie?

MARGARET:
Well, he broke it, Big Mama.

BIG MAMA:
I know he broke it.

   [*A phone is ringing in hall. A Negro voice answers:
   "Mistuh Polly's res'dence."*]

I mean does it hurt him much still.

MARGARET:
I'm afraid I can't give you that information, Big Mama.
You'll have to ask Brick if it hurts much still or not.

SOOKEY [*in the hall*]:
It's Memphis, Mizz Polly, it's Miss Sally in Memphis.

BIG MAMA:
Awright, Sookey.

> [*Big Mama rushes into the hall and is heard shouting
> on the phone:*]

Hello, Miss Sally. How are you, Miss Sally?—Yes, well,
I was just gonna call you about it. *Shoot!*—

> [*She raises her voice to a bellow.*]

*Miss Sally? Don't ever call me from the Gayoso Lobby,
too much talk goes on in that hotel lobby, no wonder
you can't hear me!* Now listen, Miss Sally. They's nothin'
serious wrong with Big Daddy. We got the report just
now, they's nothin' wrong but a thing called a—spastic!
SPASTIC!—colon . . .

> [*She appears at the hall door and calls to Margaret.*]

—Maggie, come out here and talk to that fool on the
phone. I'm shouted breathless!

MARGARET [*goes out and is heard sweetly at phone*]:
Miss Sally? This is Brick's wife, Maggie. So nice to hear
your voice. Can you hear *mine?* Well, *good!*—Big Mama
just wanted you to know that they've got the report from
the Ochsner Clinic and what Big Daddy has is a spastic
colon. Yes. Spastic colon, Miss Sally. That's right, spastic
colon. *G'bye, Miss Sally, hope I'll see you real soon!*

> [*Hangs up a little before Miss Sally was probably
> ready to terminate the talk. She returns through the
> hall door.*]

She heard me perfectly. I've discovered with deaf people
the thing to do is not shout at them but just enunciate
clearly. My rich old Aunt Cornelia was deaf as the dead
but I could make her hear me just by sayin' each word
slowly, distinctly, close to her ear. I read her the *Com-
mercial Appeal* ev'ry night, read her the classified ads in

it, even, she never missed a word of it. But was she a mean ole thing! Know what I got when she died? Her unexpired subscriptions to five magazines and the Book-of-the-Month Club and a LIBRARY full of ev'ry dull book ever written! All else went to her hellcat of a sister . . . meaner than she was, even!

[*Big Mama has been straightening things up in the room during this speech.*]

BIG MAMA [*closing closet door on discarded clothes*]:
Miss Sally sure is a case! Big Daddy says she's always got her hand out fo' something. He's not mistaken. That poor ole thing always has her hand out fo' somethin'. I don't think Big Daddy gives her as much as he should.

[*Somebody shouts for her downstairs and she shouts:*]
I'm comin'!

[*She starts out. At the hall door, turns and jerks a forefinger, first toward the bathroom door, then toward the liquor cabinet, meaning: "Has Brick been drinking?" Margaret pretends not to understand, cocks her head and raises her brows as if the panto-mimic performance was completely mystifying to her. [Big Mama rushes back to Margaret:*]

Shoot! Stop playin' so dumb!—I mean has he been drinkin' that stuff much yet?

MARGARET [*with a little laugh*]:
Oh! I think he had a highball after supper.

BIG MAMA:
Don't laugh about it!—Some single men stop drinkin' when they git married and others start! Brick never touched liquor before he—!

MARGARET [*crying out*]:
THAT'S NOT FAIR!

BIG MAMA:
Fair or not fair I want to ask you a question, one question: D'you make Brick happy in bed?

MARGARET:
Why don't you ask if he makes *me* happy in bed?

BIG MAMA:
Because I know that—

MARGARET:
It works both ways!

BIG MAMA:
Something's not right! You're childless and my son
drinks!

> [*Someone has called her downstairs and she has
> rushed to the door on the line above. She turns at
> the door and points at the bed.*]

—When a marriage goes on the rocks, the rocks are
there, right *there!*

MARGARET:
That's—

> [*Big Mama has swept out of the room and slammed
> the door.*]

—not—*fair . . .*

> [*Margaret is alone, completely alone, and she feels it.
> She draws in, hunches her shoulders, raises her arms
> with fists clenched, shuts her eyes tight as a child
> about to be stabbed with a vaccination needle. When
> she opens her eyes again, what she sees is the long
> oval mirror and she rushes straight to it, stares into
> it with a grimace and says: "Who are you?"—Then
> she crouches a little and answers herself in a different
> voice which is high, thin, mocking: "I am Maggie the
> Cat!"—Straightens quickly as bathroom door opens
> a little and Brick calls out to her.*]

BRICK:
Has Big Mama gone?

MARGARET:
She's gone.

> [*He opens the bathroom door and hobbles out, with
> his liquor glass now empty, straight to the liquor cab-
> inet. He is whistling softly. Margaret's head pivots on
> her long, slender throat to watch him.*
> [*She raises a hand uncertainly to the base of her*

throat, as if it was difficult for her to swallow, before she speaks:]

You know, our sex life didn't just peter out in the usual way, it was cut off short, long before the natural time for it to, and it's going to revive again, just as sudden as that. I'm confident of it. That's what I'm keeping myself attractive for. For the time when you'll see me again like other men see me. Yes, like other men see me. They still see me, Brick, and they like what they see. Uh-huh. Some of them would give their—
Look, Brick!

[She stands before the long oval mirror, touches her breast and then her hips with her two hands.]

How high my body stays on me!—Nothing has fallen on me—not a fraction. . . .

[Her voice is soft and trembling: a pleading child's. At this moment as he turns to glance at her—a look which is like a player passing a ball to another player, third down and goal to go—she has to capture the audience in a grip so tight that she can hold it till the first intermission without any lapse of attention.]

Other men still want me. My face looks strained, sometimes, but I've kept my figure as well as you've kept yours, and men admire it. I still turn heads on the street. Why, last week in Memphis everywhere that I went men's eyes burned holes in my clothes, at the country club and in restaurants and department stores, there wasn't a man I met or walked by that didn't just eat me up with his eyes and turn around when I passed him and look back at me. Why, at Alice's party for her New York cousins, the best lookin' man in the crowd—followed me upstairs and tried to force his way in the powder room with me, followed me to the door and tried to force his way in!

BRICK:
Why didn't you let him, Maggie?

MARGARET:
Because I'm not that common, for one thing. Not that I

wasn't almost tempted to. You like to know who it was? It was Sonny Boy Maxwell, that's who!

BRICK:
Oh, yeah, Sonny Boy Maxwell, he was a good end-runner but had a little injury to his back and had to quit.

MARGARET:
He has no injury now and has no wife and still has a lech for me!

BRICK:
I see no reason to lock him out of a powder room in that case.

MARGARET:
And have someone catch me at it? I'm not that stupid. Oh, I might sometime cheat on you with someone, since you're so insultingly eager to have me do it!—But if I do, you can be damned sure it will be in a place and a time where no one but me and the man could possibly know. Because I'm not going to give you any excuse to divorce me for being unfaithful or anything else. . . .

BRICK:
Maggie, I wouldn't divorce you for being unfaithful or anything else. Don't you know that? Hell. I'd be relieved to know that you'd found yourself a lover.

MARGARET:
Well, I'm taking no chances. No, I'd rather stay on this hot tin roof.

BRICK:
A hot tin roof's 'n uncomfo'table place t' stay on. . . .
    [*He starts to whistle softly.*]

MARGARET [*through his whistle*]:
Yeah, but I can stay on it just as long as I have to.

BRICK:
You could leave me, Maggie.
    [*He resumes whistle. She wheels about to glare at him.*]

MARGARET:

Don't want to and will not! Besides if I did, you don't have a cent to pay for it but what you get from Big Daddy and he's dying of cancer!

[*For the first time a realization of Big Daddy's doom seems to penetrate to Brick's consciousness, visibly, and he looks at Margaret.*]

BRICK:

Big Mama just said he *wasn't,* that the report was okay.

MARGARET:

That's what she thinks because she got the same story that they gave Big Daddy. And was just as taken in by it as he was, poor ole things. . . .
But tonight they're going to tell her the truth about it. When Big Daddy goes to bed, they're going to tell her that he is dying of cancer.

[*She slams the dresser drawer.*]

—It's malignant and it's terminal.

BRICK:

Does Big Daddy know it?

MARGARET:

Hell, do they *ever* know it? Nobody says, "You're dying." You have to fool them. They have to fool *themselves.*

BRICK:

Why?

MARGARET:

Why? Because human beings dream of life everlasting, that's the reason! But most of them want it on earth and not in heaven.

[*He gives a short, hard laugh at her touch of humor.*]

Well. . . . [*She touches up her mascara.*] That's how it is, anyhow. . . . [*She looks about.*] Where did I put down my cigarette? Don't want to burn up the home-place, at least not with Mae and Gooper and their five monsters in it!

[*She has found it and sucks at it greedily. Blows out smoke and continues:*]

So this is Big Daddy's last birthday. And Mae and Gooper, they know it, oh, *they* know it, all right. They got the first information from the Ochsner Clinic. That's why they rushed down here with their no-neck monsters. Because. Do you know something? Big Daddy's made no will? Big Daddy's never made out any will in his life, and so this campaign's afoot to impress him, forcibly as possible, with the fact that you drink and I've borne no children!

[*He continues to stare at her a moment, then mutters something sharp but not audible and hobbles rather rapidly out onto the long gallery in the fading, much faded, gold light.*]

MARGARET [*continuing her liturgical chant*]:
Y'know, I'm *fond* of Big Daddy, I am genuinely fond of that old man, I really *am*, you know. . . .

BRICK [*faintly, vaguely*]:
Yes, I know you are. . . .

MARGARET:
I've always sort of admired him in spite of his coarseness, his four-letter words and so forth. Because Big Daddy *is* what he *is*, and he makes no bones about it. He hasn't turned gentleman farmer, he's still a Mississippi red neck, as much of a red neck as he must have been when he was just overseer here on the old Jack Straw and Peter Ochello place. But he got hold of it an' built it into th' biggest an' finest plantation in the Delta.—I've always *liked* Big Daddy. . . .

[*She crosses to the proscenium.*]

Well, this is Big Daddy's last birthday. I'm sorry about it. But I'm facing the facts. It takes money to take care of a drinker and that's the office that I've been elected to lately.

BRICK:
You don't have to take care of me.

MARGARET:
Yes, I do. Two people in the same boat have got to take
care of each other. At least you want money to buy
more Echo Spring when this supply is exhausted, or will
you be satisfied with a ten-cent beer?
Mae an' Gooper are plannin' to freeze us out of Big
Daddy's estate because you drink and I'm childless. But
we can defeat that plan. We're *going* to defeat that plan!
*Brick, y'know, I've been so goddam disgustingly poor all
my life!*—That's the *truth*, Brick!

BRICK:
I'm not sayin' it isn't.

MARGARET:
Always had to suck up to people I couldn't stand because they had money and I was poor as Job's turkey.
You don't know what that's like. Well, I'll tell you, it's
like you would feel a thousand miles away from Echo
Spring!—And had to get back to it on that broken
ankle . . . without a crutch!
That's how it feels to be as poor as Job's turkey and
have to suck up to relatives that you hated because they
had money and all you had was a bunch of hand-me-
down clothes and a few old moldy three per cent government bonds. My daddy loved his liquor, he fell in love
with his liquor the way you've fallen in love with Echo
Spring!—And my poor mama, having to maintain some
semblance of social position, to keep appearances up, on
an income of one hundred and fifty dollars a month on
those old government bonds!
When I came out, the year that I made my debut, I had
just two evening dresses! One Mother made me from a
pattern in *Vogue,* the other a hand-me-down from a
snotty rich cousin I hated!
—The dress that I married you in was my grandmother's
weddin' gown. . . .
So that's why I'm like a cat on a hot tin roof!

[*Brick is still on the gallery. Someone below calls up
to him in a warm Negro voice, "Hiya, Mistuh Brick,*

*how yuh feelin'?" Brick raises his liquor glass as if
that answered the question.*]

You can be young without money but you can't be old
without it. You've got to be old *with* money because to
be old without it is just too awful, you've got to be one
or the other, either *young* or *with money,* you can't be
old and *without* it.—That's the truth, Brick. . . .

[*Brick whistles softly, vaguely.*]

Well, now I'm dressed, I'm all dressed, there's nothing
else for me to do.

[*Forlornly, almost fearfully.*]

I'm dressed, all dressed, nothing else for me to do. . . .

[*She moves about restlessly, aimlessly, and speaks, as
if to herself.*]

I know when I made my mistake.—What am I—? Oh!—
my bracelets. . . .

[*She starts working a collection of bracelets over her
hands onto her wrists, about six on each, as she
talks.*]

I've thought a whole lot about it and now I know when
I made my mistake. Yes, I made my mistake when I told
you the truth about that thing with Skipper. Never
should have confessed it, a fatal error, tellin' you about
that thing with Skipper.

BRICK:
Maggie, shut up about Skipper. I mean it, Maggie; you
got to shut up about Skipper.

MARGARET:
You ought to understand that Skipper and I—

BRICK:
You don't think I'm serious, Maggie? You're fooled by
the fact that I am saying this quiet? Look, Maggie. What
you're doing is a dangerous thing to do. You're—
you're—you're—foolin' with something that—nobody
ought to fool with.

MARGARET:
This time I'm going to finish what I have to say to you.

Skipper and I made love, if love you could call it, because it made both of us feel a little bit closer to you.
You see, you son of a bitch, you asked too much of
people, of me, of him, of all the unlucky poor damned
sons of bitches that happen to love you, and there was
a whole pack of them, yes, there was a pack of them
besides me and Skipper, you asked too goddam much
of people that loved you, you—superior creature!—you
godlike being!—And so we made love to each other to
dream it was you, both of us! Yes, yes, yes! Truth, truth!
What's so awful about it? I like it, I think the truth is—
yeah! I shouldn't have told you. . . .

BRICK [*holding his head unnaturally still and uptilted a
bit*]:
It was Skipper that told me about it. Not you, Maggie.

MARGARET:
I told you!

BRICK:
After he told me!

MARGARET:
What does it matter who—?
      [*Brick turns suddenly out upon the gallery and calls:*]

BRICK:
Little girl! Hey, little girl!

LITTLE GIRL [*at a distance*]:
What, Uncle Brick?

BRICK:
Tell the folks to come up!—Bring everybody upstairs!

MARGARET:
I can't stop myself! I'd go on telling you this in front of
them all, if I had to!

BRICK:
Little girl! Go on, go on, will you? Do what I told you,
call them!

MARGARET:
Because it's got to be told and you, you!—you never
let me!

[*She sobs, then controls herself, and continues almost calmly.*]

It was one of those beautiful, ideal things they tell about
in the Greek legends, it couldn't be anything else, you
being you, and that's what made it so sad, that's what
made it so awful, because it was love that never could
be carried through to anything satisfying or even talked
about plainly. Brick, I tell you, you got to believe me,
Brick, I *do* understand all about it. I—I think it was—
noble! Can't you tell I'm sincere when I say I respect
it? My only point, the only point that I'm making, is life
has got to be allowed to continue even after the *dream*
of life is—all—over. . . .

[*Brick is without his crutch. Leaning on furniture, he
crosses to pick it up as she continues as if possessed
by a will outside herself:*]

Why I remember when we double-dated at college,
Gladys Fitzgerald and I and you and Skipper, it was
more like a date between you and Skipper. Gladys and
I were just sort of tagging along as if it was necessary
to chaperone you!—to make a good public impression—

BRICK [*turns to face her, half lifting his crutch*]:
Maggie, you want me to hit you with this crutch? Don't
you know I could kill you with this crutch?

MARGARET:
Good Lord, man, d' you think I'd care if you did?

BRICK:
One man has one great good true thing in his life. One
great good thing which is true!—I had friendship with
Skipper.—You are naming it dirty!

MARGARET:
I'm not naming it dirty! I am naming it clean.

BRICK:
Not love with you, Maggie, but friendship with Skipper

was that one great true thing, and you are naming it dirty!

MARGARET:
Then you haven't been listenin', not understood what I'm saying! I'm naming it so damn clean that it killed poor Skipper!—You two had something that had to be kept on ice, yes, incorruptible, yes!—and death was the only icebox where you could keep it. . . .

BRICK:
I married you, Maggie. Why would I marry you, Maggie, if I was—?

MARGARET:
Brick, don't brain me yet, let me finish!—I know, believe me I know, that it was only Skipper that harbored even any *unconscious* desire for anything not perfectly pure between you two!—Now let me skip a little. You married me early that summer we graduated out of Ole Miss, and we were happy, weren't we, we were blissful, yes, hit heaven together ev'ry time that we loved! But that fall you an' Skipper turned down wonderful offers of jobs in order to keep on bein' football heroes—pro-football heroes. You organized the Dixie Stars that fall, so you could keep on bein' team-mates forever! But somethin' was not right with it!—*Me included!*—between you. Skipper began hittin' the bottle . . . you got a spinal injury—couldn't play the Thanksgivin' game in Chicago, watched it on TV from a traction bed in Toledo. I joined Skipper. The Dixie Stars lost because poor Skipper was drunk. We drank together that night all night in the bar of the Blackstone and when cold day was comin' up over the Lake an' we were comin' out drunk to take a dizzy look at it, I said, "SKIPPER! STOP LOVIN' MY HUS-BAND OR TELL HIM HE'S GOT TO LET YOU ADMIT IT TO HIM!"—one way or another!
HE SLAPPED ME HARD ON THE MOUTH!—then turned and ran without stopping once, I am sure, all the way back into his room at the Blackstone. . . .
—When I came to his room that night, with a little scratch like a shy little mouse at his door, he made that

pitiful, ineffectual little attempt to prove that what I had
said wasn't true. . . .

[*Brick strikes at her with crutch, a blow that shatters
the gemlike lamp on the table.*]

—In this way, I destroyed him, by telling him truth that
he and his world which he was born and raised in, yours
and his world, had told him could not be told?

—From then on Skipper was nothing at all but a recepta-
cle for liquor and drugs. . . .

—*Who shot cock-robin? I with my*—

[*She throws back her head with tight shut eyes.*]

—*merciful arrow!*

[*Brick strikes at her; misses.*]

Missed me!—Sorry,—I'm not tryin' to whitewash my behavior, Christ, no! Brick, I'm not good. I don't know
why people have to pretend to be good, nobody's good.
The rich or the well-to-do can afford to respect moral
patterns, conventional moral patterns, but I could never
afford to, yeah, but—I'm honest! Give me credit for just
that, will you *please?*—Born poor, raised poor, expect to
die poor unless I manage to get us something out of
what Big Daddy leaves when he dies of cancer! But
Brick?!—*Skipper is dead! I'm alive!* Maggie the cat is—

[*Brick hops awkwardly forward and strikes at her
again with his crutch.*]

—*alive! I am alive, alive! I am* . . .

[*He hurls the crutch at her, across the bed she took
refuge behind, and pitches forward on the floor as
she completes her speech.*]

—*alive!*

[*A little girl, Dixie, bursts into the room, wearing an
Indian war bonnet and firing a cap pistol at Margaret
and shouting: "Bang, bang, bang!"*]

[*Laughter downstairs floats through the open hall
door. Margaret had crouched gasping to bed at
child's entrance. She now rises and says with cool
fury:*]

Little girl, your mother or someone should teach you—

[*Gasping*]—to knock at a door before you come into a room. Otherwise people might think that you—lack—good breeding. . . .

DIXIE:
Yanh, yanh, yanh, what is Uncle Brick doin' on th' floor?

BRICK:
I tried to kill your Aunt Maggie, but I failed—and I fell. Little girl, give me my crutch so I can get up off th' floor.

MARGARET:
Yes, give your uncle his crutch, he's a cripple, honey, he broke his ankle last night jumping hurdles on the high school athletic field!

DIXIE:
What were you jumping hurdles for, Uncle Brick?

BRICK:
Because I used to jump them, and people like to do what they used to do, even after they've stopped being able to do it. . . .

MARGARET:
That's right, that's your answer, now go away, little girl.

[*Dixie fires cap pistol at Margaret three times.*]

Stop, you stop that, monster! You little no-neck monster!

[*She seizes the cap pistol and hurls it through gallery doors.*]

DIXIE [*with a precocious instinct for the cruelest thing*]:
You're *jealous!*—You're just jealous because you can't have babies!

[*She sticks out her tongue at Margaret as she sashays past her with her stomach stuck out, to the gallery. Margaret slams the gallery doors and leans panting against them. There is a pause. Brick has replaced his spilt drink and sits, faraway, on the great four-poster bed.*]

MARGARET:
You see?—they gloat over us being childless, even in front of their five little no-neck monsters!

[*Pause. Voices approach on the stairs.*]

Brick?—I've been to a doctor in Memphis, a—a gyne-cologist. . . .

I've been completely examined, and there is no reason why we can't have a child whenever we want one. And this is my time by the calendar to conceive. Are you listening to me? Are you? Are you LISTENING TO ME!

BRICK:
Yes. I hear you, Maggie.

[*His attention returns to her inflamed face.*]

—But how in hell on earth do you imagine—that you're going to have a child by a man that can't stand you?

MARGARET:
That's a problem that I will have to work out.

[*She wheels about to face the hall door.*]

Here they come!

[*The lights dim.*]

CURTAIN

ACT TWO

There is no lapse of time. Margaret and Brick are in the same positions they held at the end of Act I.

MARGARET [*at door*]:
Here they come!

> [*Big Daddy appears first, a tall man with a fierce, anxious look, moving carefully not to betray his weakness even, or especially, to himself.*]

BIG DADDY:
Well, Brick.

BRICK:
Hello, Big Daddy.—Congratulations!

BIG DADDY:
—Crap. . . .

> [*Some of the people are approaching through the hall, others along the gallery: voices from both directions. Gooper and Reverend Tooker become visible outside gallery doors, and their voices come in clearly.*
> [*They pause outside as Gooper lights a cigar.*]

REVEREND TOOKER [*vivaciously*]:
Oh, but St. Paul's in Grenada has three memorial windows, and the latest one is a Tiffany stained-glass window that cost twenty-five hundred dollars, a picture of Christ the Good Shepherd with a Lamb in His arms.

GOOPER:
Who give that window, Preach?

REVEREND TOOKER:
Clyde Fletcher's widow. Also presented St. Paul's with
a baptismal font.

GOOPER:
Y'know what somebody ought t' give your church is a
coolin' system, Preach.

REVEREND TOOKER:
Yes, siree, Bob! And y'know what Gus Hamma's family
gave in his memory to the church at Two Rivers? A
complete new stone parish-house with a basketball court
in the basement and a—

BIG DADDY [*uttering a loud barking laugh which is far
from truly mirthful*]:
Hey, Preach! What's all this talk about memorials,
Preach? Y' think somebody's about t' kick off around
here? 'S that it?

> [*Startled by this interjection, Reverend Tooker de-
> cides to laugh at the question almost as loud as he
> can.*
> [*How he would answer the question we'll never
> know, as he's spared that embarrassment by the voice
> of Gooper's wife, Mae, rising high and clear as she
> appears with "Doc" Baugh, the family doctor,
> through the hall door.*]

MAE [*almost religiously*]:
—Let's see now, they've had their *tyyy*-phoid shots, and
their tetanus shots, their diphtheria shots and their hepa-
titis shots and their polio shots, they got *those* shots
every month from May through September, and—
Gooper? Hey! Gooper!—What all have the kiddies been
shot faw?

MARGARET [*overlapping a bit*]:
Turn on the Hi-Fi, Brick! Let's have some music t' start
off th' party with!

> [*The talk becomes so general that the room sounds
> like a great aviary of chattering birds. Only Brick
> remains unengaged, leaning upon the liquor cabinet
> with his faraway smile, an ice cube in a paper napkin*

*with which he now and then rubs his forehead. He
doesn't respond to Margaret's command. She bounds
forward and stoops over the instrument panel of
the console.*]

GOOPER:
We gave 'em that thing for a third anniversary present,
got three speakers in it.

[*The room is suddenly blasted by the climax of a
Wagnerian opera or a Beethoven symphony.*]

BIG DADDY:
Turn that dam thing off!

[*Almost instant silence, almost instantly broken by
the shouting charge of Big Mama, entering through
hall door like a charging rhino.*]

BIG MAMA:
Wha's my Brick, wha's mah precious baby!!

BIG DADDY:
Sorry! Turn it back on!

[*Everyone laughs very loud. Big Daddy is famous
for his jokes at Big Mama's expense, and nobody
laughs louder at these jokes than Big Mama herself,
though sometimes they're pretty cruel and Big Mama
has to pick up or fuss with something to cover the
hurt that the loud laugh doesn't quite cover.*
[*On this occasion, a happy occasion because the
dread in her heart has also been lifted by the false
report on Big Daddy's condition, she giggles, gro-
tesquely, coyly, in Big Daddy's direction and bears
down upon Brick, all very quick and alive.*]

BIG MAMA:
Here he is, here's my precious baby! What's that you've
got in your hand? You put that liquor down, son, your
hand was made fo' holdin' somethin' better than that!

GOOPER:
Look at Brick put it down!

[*Brick has obeyed Big Mama by draining the glass*

and handing it to her. Again everyone laughs, some high, some low.]

BIG MAMA:

Oh, you bad boy, you, you're my bad little boy. Give Big Mama a kiss, you bad boy, you!—Look at him shy away, will you? Brick never liked bein' kissed or made a fuss over, I guess because he's always had too much of it!

Son, you turn that thing off!

[*Brick has switched on the TV set.*]

I can't stand TV, radio was bad enough but TV has gone it one better, I mean—[*Plops wheezing in chair*]—one worse, ha ha! Now what'm I sittin' down here faw? I want t' sit next to my sweetheart on the sofa, hold hands with him and love him up a little!

[*Big Mama has on a black and white figured chiffon. The large irregular patterns, like the markings of some massive animal, the luster of her great diamonds and many pearls, the brilliants set in the silver frames of her glasses, her riotous voice, booming laugh, have dominated the room since she entered. Big Daddy has been regarding her with a steady grimace of chronic annoyance.*]

BIG MAMA [*still louder*]:

Preacher, Preacher, hey, Preach! Give me you' hand an' help me up from this chair!

REVEREND TOOKER:

None of your tricks, Big Mama!

BIG MAMA:

What tricks? You give me you' hand so I can get up an'—

[*Reverend Tooker extends her his hand. She grabs it and pulls him into her lap with a shrill laugh that spans an octave in two notes.*]

Ever seen a preacher in a fat lady's lap? Hey, hey, folks! Ever seen a preacher in a fat lady's lap?

[*Big Mama is notorious throughout the Delta for this*]

*sort of inelegant horseplay. Margaret looks on with
indulgent humor, sipping Dubonnet "on the rocks"
and watching Brick, but Mae and Gooper exchange
signs of humorless anxiety over these antics, the sort
of behavior which Mae thinks may account for their
failure to quite get in with the smartest young married
set in Memphis, despite all. One of the Negroes,
Lacey or Sookey, peeks in, cackling. They are waiting for a sign to bring in the cake and champagne.
But Big Daddy's not amused. He doesn't understand
why, in spite of the infinite mental relief he's received
from the doctor's report, he still has these same old
fox teeth in his guts. "This spastic thing sure is something," he says to himself, but aloud he roars at
Big Mama:]*

BIG DADDY:
BIG MAMA, WILL YOU QUIT HORSIN'?—You're
too old an' too fat fo' that sort of crazy kid stuff an'
besides a woman with your blood-pressure—she had two
hundred last spring!—is riskin' a stroke when you mess
around like that. . . .

BIG MAMA:
Here comes Big Daddy's birthday!

*[Negroes in white jackets enter with an enormous
birthday cake ablaze with candles and carrying buck-
ets of champagne with satin ribbons about the bottle necks.
[Mae and Gooper strike up song, and everybody,
including the Negroes and Children, joins in. Only
Brick remains aloof.]*

EVERYONE:
Happy birthday to you.
Happy birthday to you.
Happy birthday, Big Daddy—
[Some sing: "Dear, Big Daddy!"]
Happy birthday to you.
*[Some sing: "How old are you?"
[Mae has come down center and is organizing her*

children like a chorus. She gives them a barely audible: "One, two, three!" and they are off in the new tune.]

CHILDREN:
Skinamarinka—dinka—dink
Skinamarinka—do
We love you.
Skinamarinka—dinka—dink
Skinamarinka—do

[*All together, they turn to Big Daddy.*]

Big Daddy, you!

[*They turn back front, like a musical comedy chorus.*]

We love you in the morning;
We love you in the night.
We love you when we're with you,
And we love you out of sight.
Skinamarinka—dinka—dink
Skinamarinka—do.

[*Mae turns to Big Mama.*]

Big Mama, too!

[*Big Mama bursts into tears. The Negroes leave.*]

BIG DADDY:
Now Ida, what the hell is the matter with you?

MAE:
She's just so happy.

BIG MAMA:
I'm just so happy, Big Daddy, I have to cry or something.

[*Sudden and loud in the hush:*]

Brick, do you know the wonderful news that Doc Baugh got from the clinic about Big Daddy? Big Daddy's one hundred per cent!

MARGARET:
Isn't that wonderful?

BIG MAMA:
He's just one hundred per cent. Passed the examination
with flying colors. Now that we know there's nothing
wrong with Big Daddy but a spastic colon, I can tell you
something. I was worried sick, half out of my mind, for
fear that Big Daddy might have a thing like—

> [*Margaret cuts through this speech, jumping up and
> exclaiming shrilly:*]

MARGARET:
Brick, honey, aren't you going to give Big Daddy his
birthday present?

> [*Passing by him, she snatches his liquor glass from
> him.*
> [*She picks up a fancily wrapped package.*]

Here it is, Big Daddy, this is from Brick!

BIG MAMA:
This is the biggest birthday Big Daddy's ever had, a
hundred presents and bushels of telegrams from—

MAE [*at same time*]:
What is it, Brick?

GOOPER:
I bet 500 to 50 that Brick don't *know* what it is.

BIG MAMA:
The fun of presents is not knowing what they are till
you open the package. Open your present, Big Daddy.

BIG DADDY:
Open it you'self. I want to ask Brick somethin'! Come
here, Brick.

MARGARET:
Big Daddy's callin' you, Brick.

> [*She is opening the package.*]

BRICK:
Tell Big Daddy I'm crippled.

BIG DADDY:
I see you're crippled. I want to know how you got
crippled.

MARGARET [*making diversionary tactics*]:
Oh, look, oh, look, why, it's a cashmere robe!

[*She holds the robe up for all to see.*]

MAE:
You sound surprised, Maggie.

MARGARET:
I never saw one before.

MAE:
That's funny.—*Hah!*

MARGARET [*turning on her fiercely, with a brilliant smile*]:
Why is it funny? All my family ever had was family—
and luxuries such as cashmere robes still surprise me!

BIG DADDY [*ominously*]:
Quiet!

MAE [*heedless in her fury*]:
I don't see how you could be so surprised when you
bought it yourself at Loewenstein's in Memphis last Sat-
urday. You know how I know?

BIG DADDY:
I said, Quiet!

MAE:
—I know because the salesgirl that sold it to you waited
on me and said, Oh, Mrs. Pollitt, your sister-in-law just
bought a cashmere robe for your husband's father!

MARGARET:
Sister Woman! Your talents are wasted as a housewife
and mother, you really ought to be with the FBI or—

BIG DADDY:
QUIET!

[*Reverend Tooker's reflexes are slower than the others'. He finishes a sentence after the bellow.*]

REVEREND TOOKER [*to Doc Baugh*]:
—the Stork and the Reaper are running neck and neck!

[*He starts to laugh gaily when he notices the silence and Big Daddy's glare. His laugh dies falsely.*]

BIG DADDY:
Preacher, I hope I'm not butting in on more talk about memorial stained-glass windows, am I, Preacher?

[*Reverend Tooker laughs feebly, then coughs dryly in the embarrassed silence.*]

Preacher?

BIG MAMA:
Now, Big Daddy, don't you pick on Preacher!

BIG DADDY [*raising his voice*]:
You ever hear that expression all hawk and no spit? You bring that expression to mind with that little dry cough of yours, all hawk an' no spit. . . .

[*The pause is broken only by a short startled laugh from Margaret, the only one there who is conscious of and amused by the grotesque.*]

MAE [*raising her arms and jangling her bracelets*]:
I wonder if the mosquitoes are active tonight?

BIG DADDY:
What's that, Little Mama? Did you make some remark?

MAE:
Yes, I said I wondered if the mosquitoes would eat us alive if we went out on the gallery for a while.

BIG DADDY:
Well, if they do, I'll have your bones pulverized for fertilizer!

BIG MAMA [*quickly*]:
Last week we had an airplane spraying the place and I think it done some good, at least I haven't had a—

BIG DADDY [*cutting her speech*]:
Brick, they tell me, if what they tell me is true, that you done some jumping last night on the high school athletic field?

BIG MAMA:
Brick, Big Daddy is talking to you, son.

BRICK [*smiling vaguely over his drink*]:
What was that, Big Daddy?

BIG DADDY:
They said you done some jumping on the high school track field last night.

BRICK:
That's what they told me, too.

BIG DADDY:
Was it jumping or humping that you were doing out there? What were you doing out there at three a.m., layin' a woman on that cinder track?

BIG MAMA:
Big Daddy, you are off the sick-list, now, and I'm not going to excuse you for talkin' so—

BIG DADDY:
Quiet!

BIG MAMA:
—*nasty* in front of Preacher and—

BIG DADDY:
QUIET!—I ast you, Brick, if you was cuttin' you'self a piece o' poon-tang last night on that cinder track? I thought maybe you were chasin' poon-tang on that track an' tripped over something in the heat of the chase— 'sthat it?

[*Gooper laughs, loud and false, others nervously following suit. Big Mama stamps her foot, and purses her lips, crossing to Mae and whispering something to her as Brick meets his father's hard, intent, grinning stare with a slow, vague smile that he offers all situations from behind the screen of his liquor.*]

BRICK:
No, sir, I don't think so. . . .

MAE [*at the same time, sweetly*]:
Reverend Tooker, let's you and I take a stroll on the widow's walk.

> [*She and the preacher go out on the gallery as Big Daddy says:*]

BIG DADDY:
Then what the hell were you doing out there at three o'clock in the morning?

BRICK:
Jumping the hurdles, Big Daddy, runnin' and jumpin' the hurdles, but those high hurdles have gotten too high for me, now.

BIG DADDY:
Cause you was drunk?

BRICK [*his vague smile fading a little*]:
Sober I wouldn't have tried to jump the *low* ones. . . .

BIG MAMA [*quickly*]:
Big Daddy, blow out the candles on your birthday cake!

MARGARET [*at the same time*]:
I want to propose a toast to Big Daddy Pollitt on his sixty-fifth birthday, the biggest cotton-planter in—

BIG DADDY [*bellowing with fury and disgust*]:
I told you to stop it, now stop it, quit this—!

BIG MAMA [*coming in front of Big Daddy with the cake*]:
Big Daddy, I will not allow you to talk that way, not even on your birthday, I—

BIG DADDY:
I'll talk like I want to on my birthday, Ida, or any other goddam day of the year and anybody here that don't like it knows what they can do!

BIG MAMA:
You don't mean that!

BIG DADDY:
What makes you think I don't mean it?

> [*Meanwhile various discreet signals have been ex-*

changed and Gooper has also gone out on the gallery.]

BIG MAMA:
I just know you don't mean it.

BIG DADDY:
You don't know a goddam thing and you never did!

BIG MAMA:
Big Daddy, you don't mean that.

BIG DADDY:
Oh, yes, I do, oh, yes, I do, I mean it! I put up with a whole lot of crap around here because I thought I was dying. And you thought I was dying and you started taking over, well, you can stop taking over now, Ida, because I'm not gonna die, you can just stop now this business of taking over because you're not taking over because I'm not dying, I went through the laboratory and the goddam exploratory operation and there's nothing wrong with me but a spastic colon. And I'm not dying of cancer which you thought I was dying of. Ain't that so? Didn't you think that I was dying of cancer, Ida?

[*Almost everybody is out on the gallery but the two old people glaring at each other across the blazing cake.*
[*Big Mama's chest heaves and she presses a fat fist to her mouth.*
[*Big Daddy continues, hoarsely:*]

Ain't that so, Ida? Didn't you have an idea I was dying of cancer and now you could take control of this place and everything on it? I got that impression, I seemed to get that impression. Your loud voice everywhere, your fat old body butting in here and there!

BIG MAMA:
Hush! The Preacher!

BIG DADDY:
Rut the goddam preacher!

[*Big Mama gasps loudly and sits down on the sofa which is almost too small for her.*]

Did you hear what I said? I said rut the goddam preacher!

[*Somebody closes the gallery doors from outside just as there is a burst of fireworks and excited cries from the children.*]

BIG MAMA:
I never seen you act like this before and I can't think what's got in you!

BIG DADDY:
I went through all that laboratory and operation and all just so I would know if you or me was boss here! Well, now it turns out that I am and you ain't—and that's my birthday present—and my cake and champagne!—because for three years now you been gradually taking over. Bossing. Talking. Sashaying your fat old body around the place I made! I made this place! I was overseer on it! I was the overseer on the old Straw and Ochello plantation. I quit school at ten! I quit school at ten years old and went to work like a nigger in the fields. And I rose to be overseer of the Straw and Ochello plantation. And old Straw died and I was Ochello's partner and the place got bigger and bigger and bigger and bigger and bigger! I did all that myself with no goddam help from you, and now you think you're just about to take over. Well, I am just about to tell you that you are not just about to take over, you are not just about to take over a goddam thing. Is that clear to you, Ida? Is that very plain to you, now? Is that understood completely? I been through the laboratory from A to Z. I've had the goddam exploratory operation, and nothing is wrong with me but a spastic colon—made spastic, I guess, by *disgust!* By all the goddam lies and liars that I have had to put up with, and all the goddam hypocrisy that I lived with all these forty years that we been livin' together!
Hey! Ida!! Blow out the candles on the birthday cake!

Purse up your lips and draw a deep breath and blow out the goddam candles on the cake!

BIG MAMA:
Oh, Big Daddy, oh, oh, oh, Big Daddy!

BIG DADDY:
What's the matter with you?

BIG MAMA:
In all these years you never believed that I loved you??

BIG DADDY:
Huh?

BIG MAMA:
And I did, I did so much, I did love you!—I even loved your hate and your hardness, Big Daddy!

> [*She sobs and rushes awkwardly out onto the gallery.*]

BIG DADDY [*to himself*]:
Wouldn't it be funny if that was true. . . .

> [*A pause is followed by a burst of light in the sky from the fireworks.*]

BRICK! HEY, BRICK!

> [*He stands over his blazing birthday cake.*
> [*After some moments, Brick hobbles in on his crutch, holding his glass.*
> [*Margaret follows him with a bright, anxious smile.*]

I didn't call you, Maggie. I called Brick.

MARGARET:
I'm just delivering him to you.

> [*She kisses Brick on the mouth which he immediately wipes with the back of his hand. She flies girlishly back out. Brick and his father are alone.*]

BIG DADDY:
Why did you do that?

BRICK:
Do what, Big Daddy?

BIG DADDY:
Wipe her kiss off your mouth like she'd spit on you.

BRICK:
I don't know. I wasn't conscious of it.

BIG DADDY:
That woman of yours has a better shape on her than Gooper's but somehow or other they got the same look about them.

BRICK:
What sort of look is that, Big Daddy?

BIG DADDY:
I don't know how to describe it but it's the same look.

BRICK:
They don't look peaceful, do they?

BIG DADDY:
No, they sure in hell don't.

BRICK:
They look nervous as cats?

BIG DADDY:
That's right, they look nervous as cats.

BRICK:
Nervous as a couple of cats on a hot tin roof?

BIG DADDY:
That's right, boy, they look like a couple of cats on a hot tin roof. It's funny that you and Gooper being so different would pick out the same type of woman.

BRICK:
Both of us married into society, Big Daddy.

BIG DADDY:
Crap . . . I wonder what gives them both that look?

BRICK:
Well. They're sittin' in the middle of a big piece of land, Big Daddy, twenty-eight thousand acres is a pretty big piece of land and so they're squaring off on it, each

determined to knock off a bigger piece of it than the
other whenever you let it go.

BIG DADDY:
I got a surprise for those women. I'm not gonna let it
go for a long time yet if that's what they're waiting for.

BRICK:
That's right, Big Daddy. You just sit tight and let them
scratch each other's eyes out. . . .

BIG DADDY:
You bet your life I'm going to sit tight on it and let
those sons of bitches scratch their eyes out, ha ha ha. . . .
But Gooper's wife's a good breeder, you got to admit she's
fertile. Hell, at supper tonight she had them all at the table
and they had to put a couple of extra leafs in the table to
make room for them, she's got five head of them, now,
and another one's comin'.

BRICK:
Yep, number six is comin'. . . .

BIG DADDY:
Brick, you know, I swear to God, I don't know the way
it happens?

BRICK:
The way what happens, Big Daddy?

BIG DADDY:
You git you a piece of land, by hook or crook, an' things
start growin' on it, things accumulate on it, and the first
thing you know it's completely out of hand, completely
out of hand!

BRICK:
Well, they say nature hates a vacuum, Big Daddy.

BIG DADDY:
That's what they say, but sometimes I think that a vacuum is a hell of a lot better than some of the stuff that
nature replaces it with.
Is someone out there by that door?

BRICK:
Yep.

BIG DADDY:
Who?

> [*He has lowered his voice.*]

BRICK:
Someone int'rested in what we say to each other.

BIG DADDY:
Gooper?——*GOOPER!*

> [*After a discreet pause, Mae appears in the gallery door.*]

MAE:
Did you call Gooper, Big Daddy?

BIG DADDY:
Aw, it was you.

MAE:
Do you want Gooper, Big Daddy?

BIG DADDY:
No, and I don't want you. I want some privacy here, while I'm having a confidential talk with my son Brick. Now it's too hot in here to close them doors, but if I have to close those rutten doors in order to have a private talk with my son Brick, just let me know and I'll close 'em. Because I hate eavesdroppers, I don't like any kind of sneakin' an' spyin'.

MAE:
Why, Big Daddy—

BIG DADDY:
You stood on the wrong side of the moon, it threw your shadow!

MAE:
I was just—

BIG DADDY:
You was just nothing but *spyin'* an' you *know* it!

MAE [*begins to sniff and sob*]:
Oh, Big Daddy, you're so unkind for some reason to those that really love you!

BIG DADDY:
Shut up, shut up, shut up! I'm going to move you and Gooper out of that room next to this! It's none of your goddam business what goes on in here at night between Brick an' Maggie. You listen at night like a couple of rutten peek-hole spies and go and give a report on what you hear to Big Mama an' she comes to me and says they say such and such and so and so about what they heard goin' on between Brick an' Maggie, and Jesus, it makes me sick. I'm goin' to move you an' Gooper out of that room, I can't stand sneakin' an' spyin', it makes me sick. . . .

[*Mae throws back her head and rolls her eyes heavenward and extends her arms as if invoking God's pity for this unjust martyrdom; then she presses a handkerchief to her nose and flies from the room with a loud swish of skirts.*]

BRICK [*now at the liquor cabinet*]:
They listen, do they?

BIG DADDY:
Yeah. They listen and give reports to Big Mama on what goes on in here between you and Maggie. They say that—

[*He stops as if embarrassed.*]

—You won't sleep with her, that you sleep on the sofa. Is that true or not true? If you don't like Maggie, get rid of Maggie!—What are you doin' there now?

BRICK:
Fresh'nin' up my drink.

BIG DADDY:
Son, you know you got a real liquor problem?

BRICK:
Yes, sir, yes, I know.

BIG DADDY:
Is that why you quit sports-announcing, because of this liquor problem?

BRICK:
Yes, sir, yes, sir, I guess so.
   [*He smiles vaguely and amiably at his father across his replenished drink.*]

BIG DADDY:
Son, don't guess about it, it's too important.

BRICK [*vaguely*]:
Yes, sir.

BIG DADDY:
And listen to me, don't look at the damn chandelier. . . .
   [*Pause. Big Daddy's voice is husky.*]
—Somethin' else we picked up at th' big fire-sale in Europe.
   [*Another pause.*]
Life is important. There's nothing else to hold onto. A man that drinks is throwing his life away. Don't do it, hold on to your life. There's nothing else to hold on to. . . .
Sit down over here so we don't have to raise our voices, the walls have ears in this place.

BRICK [*hobbling over to sit on the sofa beside him*]:
All right, Big Daddy.

BIG DADDY:
Quit!—how'd that come about? Some disappointment?

BRICK:
I don't know. Do you?

BIG DADDY:
I'm askin' you, goddam it! How in hell would I know if you don't?

BRICK:
I just got out there and found that I had a mouth full

of cotton. I was always two or three beats behind what
was goin' on on the field and so I—

BIG DADDY:
Quit!

BRICK [*amiably*]:
Yes, quit.

BIG DADDY:
Son?

BRICK:
Huh?

BIG DADDY [*inhales loudly and deeply from his cigar; then
bends suddenly a little forward, exhaling loudly and raising a hand to his forehead*]:
—Whew!—ha ha!—I took in too much smoke, it made
me a little light-headed. . . .

   [*The mantel clock chimes.*]
Why is it so damn hard for people to talk?

BRICK:
Yeah. . . .

   [*The clock goes on sweetly chiming till it has com-
   pleted the stroke of ten.*]
—Nice peaceful-soundin' clock, I like to hear it all
night. . . .

   [*He slides low and comfortable on the sofa; Big
   Daddy sits up straight and rigid with some unspoken
   anxiety. All his gestures are tense and jerky as he
   talks. He wheezes and pants and sniffs through his
   nervous speech, glancing quickly, shyly, from time to
   time, at his son.*]

BIG DADDY:
We got that clock the summer we wint to Europe, me
an' Big Mama on that damn Cook's Tour, never had
such an awful time in my life, I'm tellin' you, son, those
gooks over there, they gouge your eyeballs out in their
grand hotels. And Big Mama bought more stuff than
you could haul in a couple of boxcars, that's no crap.

Everywhere she wint on this whirlwind tour, she bought, bought, bought. Why, half that stuff she bought is still crated up in the cellar, under water last spring!

[*He laughs.*]

That Europe is nothin' on earth but a great big auction, that's all it is, that bunch of old worn-out places, it's just a big fire-sale, the whole rutten thing, an' Big Mama wint wild in it, why, you couldn't hold that woman with a mule's harness! Bought, bought, bought!—lucky I'm a rich man, yes siree, Bob, an' half that stuff is mildewin' in th' basement. It's lucky I'm a rich man, it sure is lucky, well, I'm a rich man, Brick, yep, I'm a mighty rich man.

[*His eyes light up for a moment.*]

Y'know how much I'm worth? Guess, Brick! Guess how much I'm worth!

[*Brick smiles vaguely over his drink.*]

Close on ten million in cash an' blue chip stocks, outside, mind you, of twenty-eight thousand acres of the richest land this side of the valley Nile!

[*A puff and crackle and the night sky blooms with an eerie greenish glow. Children shriek on the gallery.*]

But a man can't buy his life with it, he can't buy back his life with it when his life has been spent, that's one thing not offered in the Europe fire-sale or in the American markets or any markets on earth, a man can't buy his life with it, he can't buy back his life when his life is finished. . . .

That's a sobering thought, a very sobering thought, and that's a thought that I was turning over in my head, over and over and over—until today. . . .

I'm wiser and sadder, Brick, for this experience which I just gone through. They's one thing else that I remember in Europe.

BRICK:
What is that, Big Daddy?

BIG DADDY:
The hills around Barcelona in the country of Spain and

the children running over those bare hills in their bare
skins beggin' like starvin' dogs with howls and screeches,
and how fat the priests are on the streets of Barcelona,
so many of them and so fat and so pleasant, ha ha!—
Y'know I could feed that country? I got money enough
to feed that goddam country, but the human animal is
a selfish beast and I don't reckon the money I passed
out there to those howling children in the hills around
Barcelona would more than upholster one of the chairs
in this room, I mean pay to put a new cover on this
chair!

Hell, I threw them money like you'd scatter feed corn
for chickens, I threw money at them just to get rid of
them long enough to climb back into th' car and—
drive away. . . .

And then in Morocco, them Arabs, why, prostitution
begins at four or five, that's no exaggeration, why, I remember one day in Marrakech, that old walled Arab
city, I set on a broken-down wall to have a cigar, it was
fearful hot there and this Arab woman stood in the road
and looked at me till I was embarrassed, she stood stock
still in the dusty hot road and looked at me till I was
embarrassed. But listen to this. She had a naked child
with her, a little naked girl with her, barely able to tod-
dle, and after a while she set this child on the ground
and give her a push and whispered something to her.
This child come toward me, barely able t' walk, come
toddling up to me and—

Jesus, it makes you sick t' remember a thing like this!
It stuck out its hand and tried to unbutton my trousers!
That child was not yet five! Can you believe me? Or do
you think that I am making this up? I wint back to the
hotel and said to Big Mama, Git packed! We're clearing
out of this country. . . .

BRICK:
Big Daddy, you're on a talkin' jag tonight.

BIG DADDY [*ignoring this remark*]:
Yes, sir, that's how it is, the human animal is a beast
that dies but the fact that he's dying don't give him pity
for others, no, sir, it—

—Did you say something?

BRICK:
Yes.

BIG DADDY:
What?

BRICK:
Hand me over that crutch so I can get up.

BIG DADDY:
Where you goin'?

BRICK:
I'm takin' a little short trip to Echo Spring.

BIG DADDY:
To where?

BRICK:
Liquor cabinet. . . .

BIG DADDY:
Yes, sir, boy—

[*He hands Brick the crutch.*]

—the human animal is a beast that dies and if he's got money he buys and buys and buys and I think the reason he buys everything he can buy is that in the back of his mind he has the crazy hope that one of his purchases will be life everlasting!—Which it never can be. . . . The human animal is a beast that—

BRICK [*at the liquor cabinet*]:
Big Daddy, you sure are shootin' th' breeze here tonight.

[*There is a pause and voices are heard outside.*]

BIG DADDY:
I been quiet here lately, spoke not a word, just sat and stared into space. I had something heavy weighing on my mind but tonight that load was took off me. That's why I'm talking.—The sky looks diff'rent to me. . . .

BRICK:
You know what I like to hear most?

BIG DADDY:
What?

BRICK:
Solid quiet. Perfect unbroken quiet.

BIG DADDY:
Why?

BRICK:
Because it's more peaceful.

BIG DADDY:
Man, you'll hear a lot of that in the grave.

[*He chuckles agreeably.*]

BRICK:
Are you through talkin' to me?

BIG DADDY:
Why are you so anxious to shut me up?

BRICK:
Well, sir, ever so often you say to me, Brick, I want to
have a talk with you, but when we talk, it never material-
izes. Nothing is said. You sit in a chair and gas about
this and that and I look like I listen. I try to look like I
listen, but I don't listen, not much. Communication is—
awful hard between people an'—somehow between you
and me, it just don't—

BIG DADDY:
Have you ever been scared? I mean have you ever felt
downright terror of something?

[*He gets up.*]

Just one moment. I'm going to close these doors. . . .

[*He closes doors on gallery as if he were going to
tell an important secret.*]

BRICK:
What?

BIG DADDY:
Brick?

BRICK:
Huh?

BIG DADDY:
Son, I thought I had it!

BRICK:
Had what? Had what, Big Daddy?

BIG DADDY:
Cancer!

BRICK:
Oh . . .

BIG DADDY:
I thought the old man made out of bones had laid his cold and heavy hand on my shoulder!

BRICK:
Well, Big Daddy, you kept a tight mouth about it.

BIG DADDY:
A pig squeals. A man keeps a tight mouth about it, in spite of a man not having a pig's advantage.

BRICK:
What advantage is that?

BIG DADDY:
Ignorance—of mortality—is a comfort. A man don't have that comfort, he's the only living thing that conceives of death, that knows what it is. The others go without knowing which is the way that anything living should go, go without knowing, without any knowledge of it, and yet a pig squeals, but a man sometimes, he can keep a tight mouth about it. Sometimes he—

[*There is a deep, smoldering ferocity in the old man.*]

—can keep a tight mouth about it. I wonder if—

BRICK:
What, Big Daddy?

BIG DADDY:
A whiskey highball would injure this spastic condition?

BRICK:
No, sir, it might do it good.

BIG DADDY [*grins suddenly, wolfishly*]:
*Jesus, I can't tell you! The sky is open! Christ, it's open
again! It's open, boy, it's open!*

[*Brick looks down at his drink.*]

BRICK:
You feel better, Big Daddy?

BIG DADDY:
Better? Hell! I can breathe!—All of my life I been like
a doubled up fist. . . .

[*He pours a drink.*]

—Poundin', smashin', drivin'!—now I'm going to loosen
these doubled up hands and touch things *easy* with
them. . . .

[*He spreads his hands as if caressing the air.*]

You know what I'm contemplating?

BRICK [*vaguely*]:
No, sir. What are you contemplating?

BIG DADDY:
Ha ha!—*Pleasure!*—pleasure with *women!*

[*Brick's smile fades a little but lingers.*]

Brick, this stuff burns me!—

—Yes, boy. I'll tell you something that you might not
guess. I still have desire for women and this is my sixty-
fifth birthday.

BRICK:
I think that's mighty remarkable, Big Daddy.

BIG DADDY:
Remarkable?

BRICK:
Admirable, Big Daddy.

BIG DADDY:
You're damn right it is, remarkable and admirable both.
I realize now that I never had me enough. I let many

chances slip by because of scruples about it, scruples, convention—crap. . . . All that stuff is bull, bull, bull!— It took the shadow of death to make me see it. Now that shadow's lifted, I'm going to cut loose and have, what is it they call it, have me a—ball!

BRICK:
A ball, huh?

BIG DADDY:
That's right, a ball, a ball! Hell!—I slept with Big Mama till, let's see, five years ago, till I was sixty and she was fifty-eight, and never even liked her, never did!

[*The phone has been ringing down the hall. Big Mama enters, exclaiming:*]

BIG MAMA:
Don't you men hear that phone ring? I heard it way out on the gall'ry.

BIG DADDY:
There's five rooms off this front gall'ry that you could go through. Why do you go through this one?

[*Big Mama makes a playful face as she bustles out the hall door.*]

Hunh!—Why, when Big Mama goes out of a room, I can't remember what that woman looks like, but when Big Mama comes back into the room, boy, then I see what she looks like, and I wish I didn't!

[*Bends over laughing at this joke till it hurts his guts and he straightens with a grimace. The laugh subsides to a chuckle as he puts the liquor glass a little distrustfully down on the table.*
[*Brick has risen and hobbled to the gallery doors.*]

Hey! Where you goin'?

BRICK:
Out for a breather.

BIG DADDY:
Not yet you ain't. Stay here till this talk is finished, young fellow.

BRICK:
I thought it was finished, Big Daddy.

BIG DADDY:
It ain't even begun.

BRICK:
My mistake. Excuse me. I just wanted to feel that river breeze.

BIG DADDY:
Turn on the ceiling fan and set back down in that chair.
    [*Big Mama's voice rises, carrying down the hall.*]

BIG MAMA:
Miss Sally, you're a case! You're a caution, Miss Sally. Why didn't you give me a chance to explain it to you?

BIG DADDY:
Jesus, she's talking to my old maid sister again.

BIG MAMA:
Well, goodbye, now, Miss Sally. You come down real soon, Big Daddy's dying to see you! Yaisss, goodbye, Miss Sally. . . .
    [*She hangs up and bellows with mirth. Big Daddy groans and covers his ears as she approaches.*
    [*Bursting in:*]
Big Daddy, that was Miss Sally callin' from Memphis again! You know what she done, Big Daddy? She called her doctor in Memphis to git him to tell her what that spastic thing is! Ha-*HAAAA!*—And called back to tell me how relieved she was that—Hey! Let me in!
    [*Big Daddy has been holding the door half closed against her.*]

BIG DADDY:
Naw I ain't. I told you not to come and go through this room. You just back out and go through those five other rooms.

BIG MAMA:
Big Daddy? Big Daddy? Oh, Big Daddy!—You didn't mean those things you said to me, did you?

[*He shuts door firmly against her but she still calls.*]
Sweetheart? Sweetheart? Big Daddy? You didn't mean
those awful things you said to me?—I know you didn't.
I know you didn't mean those things in your heart. . . .

> [*The childlike voice fades with a sob and her heavy
> footsteps retreat down the hall. Brick has risen once
> more on his crutch and starts for the gallery again.*]

BIG DADDY:
All I ask of that woman is that she leave me alone. But
she can't admit to herself that she makes me sick. That
comes of having slept with her too many years. Should
of quit much sooner but that old woman she never got
enough of it—and I was good in bed . . . I never should
of wasted so much of it on her. . . . They say you got
just so many and each one is numbered. Well, I got a
few left in me, a few, and I'm going to pick me a good
one to spend 'em on! I'm going to pick me a choice one,
I don't care how much she costs, I'll smother her in—
minks! Ha ha! I'll strip her naked and smother her in
minks and choke her with diamonds! Ha ha! I'll strip
her naked and choke her with diamonds and smother
her with minks and hump her from hell to breakfast. *Ha
aha ha ha ha!*

MAE [*gaily at door*]:
Who's that laughin' in there?

GOOPER:
Is Big Daddy laughin' in there?

BIG DADDY:
Crap!—them two—*drips*. . . .

> [*He goes over and touches Brick's shoulder.*]

Yes, son. Brick, boy.—I'm—*happy!* I'm happy, son,
I'm happy!

> [*He chokes a little and bites his under lip, pressing
> his head quickly, shyly against his son's head and
> then, coughing with embarrassment, goes uncertainly
> back to the table where he set down the glass. He
> drinks and makes a grimace as it burns his guts.
> Brick sighs and rises with effort.*]

What makes you so restless? Have you got ants in your britches?

BRICK:
Yes, sir . . .

BIG DADDY:
Why?

BRICK:
—Something—hasn't—happened. . . .

BIG DADDY:
Yeah? What is that!

BRICK [*sadly*]:
—the click. . . .

BIG DADDY:
Did you say click?

BRICK:
Yes, click.

BIG DADDY:
What click?

BRICK:
A click that I get in my head that makes me peaceful.

BIG DADDY:
I sure in hell don't know what you're talking about, but it disturbs me.

BRICK:
It's just a mechanical thing.

BIG DADDY:
What is a mechanical thing?

BRICK:
This click that I get in my head that makes me peaceful. I got to drink till I get it. It's just a mechanical thing, something like a—like a—like a—

BIG DADDY:
Like a—

BRICK:
Switch clicking off in my head, turning the hot light off and the cool night on and—

[*He looks up, smiling sadly.*]

—all of a sudden there's—peace!

BIG DADDY [*whistles long and soft with astonishment; he goes back to Brick and clasps his son's two shoulders*]:
Jesus! I didn't know it had gotten that bad with you. Why, boy, you're—*alcoholic!*

BRICK:
That's the truth, Big Daddy. I'm alcoholic.

BIG DADDY:
This shows how I—let things go!

BRICK:
I have to hear that little click in my head that makes me peaceful. Usually I hear it sooner than this, sometimes as early as—noon, but—
—Today it's—dilatory. . . .
—I just haven't got the right level of alcohol in my bloodstream yet!

[*This last statement is made with energy as he freshens his drink.*]

BIG DADDY:
Uh—huh. Expecting death made me blind. I didn't have no idea that a son of mine was turning into a drunkard under my nose.

BRICK [*gently*]:
Well, now you do, Big Daddy, the news has penetrated.

BIG DADDY:
UH-huh, yes, now I do, the news has—penetrated. . . .

BRICK:
And so if you'll excuse me—

BIG DADDY:
No, I won't excuse you.

BRICK:
—I'd better sit by myself till I hear that click in my head, it's just a mechanical thing but it don't happen except when I'm alone or talking to no one. . . .

BIG DADDY:
You got a long, long time to sit still, boy, and talk to no one, but now you're talkin' to me. At least I'm talking to you. And you set there and listen until I tell you the conversation is over!

BRICK:
But this talk is like all the others we've ever had together in our lives! It's nowhere, nowhere!—it's—it's *painful*, Big Daddy. . . .

BIG DADDY:
All right, then let it be painful, but don't you move from that chair!—I'm going to remove that crutch. . . .

[*He seizes the crutch and tosses it across room.*]

BRICK:
I can hop on one foot, and if I fall, I can crawl!

BIG DADDY:
If you ain't careful you're gonna crawl off this plantation and then, by Jesus, you'll have to hustle your drinks along Skid Row!

BRICK:
That'll come, Big Daddy.

BIG DADDY:
Naw, it won't. You're my son and I'm going to straighten you out; now that *I'm* straightened out, I'm going to straighten out you!

BRICK:
Yeah?

BIG DADDY:
Today the report come in from Ochsner Clinic. Y'know what they told me?

[*His face glows with triumph.*]

The only thing that they could detect with all the instruments of science in that great hospital is a little spastic condition of the colon! And nerves torn to pieces by all that worry about it.

> [*A little girl bursts into room with a sparkler clutched in each fist, hops and shrieks like a monkey gone mad and rushes back out again as Big Daddy strikes at her.*
> [*Silence. The two men stare at each other. A woman laughs gaily outside.*]

I want you to know I breathed a sigh of relief almost as powerful as the Vicksburg tornado!

BRICK:
You weren't ready to go?

BIG DADDY:
GO WHERE?—crap. . . .
—When you are gone from here, boy, you are long gone and no where! The human machine is not no different from the animal machine or the fish machine or the bird machine or the reptile machine or the insect machine! It's just a whole goddam lot more complicated and consequently more trouble to keep together. Yep. I thought I had it. The earth shook under my foot, the sky come down like the black lid of a kettle and I couldn't breathe!—Today!!—that lid was lifted, I drew my first free breath in—how many years?—God!—three. . . .

> [*There is laughter outside, running footsteps, the soft, plushy sound and light of exploding rockets.*
> [*Brick stares at him soberly for a long moment; then makes a sort of startled sound in his nostrils and springs up on one foot and hops across the room to grab his crutch, swinging on the furniture for support. He gets the crutch and flees as if in horror for the gallery. His father seizes him by the sleeve of his white silk pajamas.*]

Stay here, you son of a bitch!—till I say go!

BRICK:
I can't.

BIG DADDY:
You sure in hell will, goddam it.

BRICK:
No, I can't. We talk, you talk, in—circles! We get nowhere, nowhere! It's always the same, you say you want
to talk to me and don't have a ruttin' thing to say to me!

BIG DADDY:
Nothin' to say when I'm tellin' you I'm going to live
when I thought I was dying?!

BRICK:
Oh—*that!*—Is that what you have to say to me?

BIG DADDY:
Why, you son of a bitch! Ain't that, ain't that—
important?!

BRICK:
Well, you said that, that's said, and now I—

BIG DADDY:
Now you set back down.

BRICK:
You're all balled up, you—

BIG DADDY:
I ain't balled up!

BRICK:
You are, you're all balled up!

BIG DADDY:
Don't tell me what I am, you drunken whelp! I'm going
to tear this coat sleeve off if you don't set down!

BRICK:
Big Daddy—

BIG DADDY:
Do what I tell you! I'm the boss here, now! I want you
to know I'm back in the driver's seat now!

[*Big Mama rushes in, clutching her great heaving
bosom.*]

What in hell do you want in here, Big Mama?

BIG MAMA:
Oh, Big Daddy! Why are you shouting like that? I just
cain't *stainnnnnnnd*—it. . . .

BIG DADDY [*raising the back of his hand above his head*]:
GIT!—outa here.

    [*She rushes back out, sobbing.*]

BRICK [*softly, sadly*]:
Christ. . . .

BIG DADDY [*fiercely*]:
Yeah! Christ!—is right . . .

    [*Brick breaks loose and hobbles toward the gallery.*
    [*Big Daddy jerks his crutch from under Brick so he
    steps with the injured ankle. He utters a hissing cry
    of anguish, clutches a chair and pulls it over on top
    of him on the floor.*]

Son of a—tub of—hog fat. . . .

BRICK:
Big Daddy! Give me my crutch.

    [*Big Daddy throws the crutch out of reach.*]

Give me that crutch, Big Daddy.

BIG DADDY:
Why do you drink?

BRICK:
Don't know, give me my crutch!

BIG DADDY:
You better think why you drink or give up drinking!

BRICK:
Will you please give me my crutch so I can get up off
this floor?

BIG DADDY:
First you answer my question. Why do you drink? Why
are you throwing your life away, boy, like somethin' disgusting you picked up on the street?

BRICK [*getting onto his knees*]:
Big Daddy, I'm in pain, I stepped on that foot.

BIG DADDY:
Good! I'm glad you're not too numb with the liquor in
you to feel some pain!

BRICK:
You—spilled my—drink . . .

BIG DADDY:
I'll make a bargain with you. You tell me why you drink
and I'll hand you one. I'll pour you the liquor myself
and hand it to you.

BRICK:
Why do I drink?

BIG DADDY:
Yeah! Why?

BRICK:
Give me a drink and I'll tell you.

BIG DADDY:
Tell me first!

BRICK:
I'll tell you in one word.

BIG DADDY:
What word?

BRICK:
DISGUST!
    [*The clock chimes softly, sweetly. Big Daddy gives it
    a short, outraged glance.*]
Now how about that drink?

BIG DADDY:
What are you disgusted with? You got to tell me that,
first. Otherwise being disgusted don't make no sense!

BRICK:
Give me my crutch.

BIG DADDY:
You heard me, you got to tell me what I asked you first.

BRICK:
I told you, I said to kill my disgust!

BIG DADDY:
DISGUST WITH WHAT!

BRICK:
You strike a hard bargain.

BIG DADDY:
What are you disgusted with?—an' I'll pass you the liquor.

BRICK:
I can hop on one foot, and if I fall, I can crawl.

BIG DADDY:
You want liquor that bad?

BRICK [*dragging himself up, clinging to bedstead*]:
Yeah, I want it that bad.

BIG DADDY:
If I give you a drink, will you tell me what it is you're disgusted with, Brick?

BRICK:
Yes, sir, I will try to.

　　[*The old man pours him a drink and solemnly passes
　　it to him.*
　　[*There is silence as Brick drinks.*]
Have you ever heard the word "mendacity"?

BIG DADDY:
Sure. Mendacity is one of them five-dollar words that cheap politicians throw back and forth at each other.

BRICK:
You know what it means?

BIG DADDY:
Don't it mean lying and liars?

BRICK:
Yes, sir, lying and liars.

BIG DADDY:
Has someone been lying to you?

CHILDREN [*chanting in chorus offstage*]:
We want Big Dad-dee!
We want Big Dad-dee!
 [*Gooper appears in the gallery door.*]

GOOPER:
Big Daddy, the kiddies are shouting for you out there.

BIG DADDY [*fiercely*]:
Keep out, Gooper!

GOOPER:
'Scuse *me!*
 [*Big Daddy slams the doors after Gooper.*]

BIG DADDY:
Who's been lying to you, has Margaret been lying to
you, has your wife been lying to you about something,
Brick?

BRICK:
Not her. That wouldn't matter.

BIG DADDY:
Then who's been lying to you, and what about?

BRICK:
No one single person and no one lie. . . .

BIG DADDY:
Then what, what then, for Christ's sake?

BRICK:
—The whole, the whole—thing. . . .

BIG DADDY:
Why are you rubbing your head? You got a headache?

BRICK:
No, I'm tryin' to—

BIG DADDY:

—Concentrate, but you can't because your brain's all soaked with liquor, is that the trouble? Wet brain!

[*He snatches the glass from Brick's hand.*]

What do you know about this mendacity thing? Hell! I could write a book on it! Don't you know that? I could write a book on it and still not cover the subject? Well, I could, I could write a goddam book on it and still not cover the subject anywhere near enough!!—Think of all the lies I got to put up with!—Pretenses! Ain't that mendacity? Having to pretend stuff you don't think or feel or have any idea of? Having for instance to act like I care for Big Mama!—I haven't been able to stand the sight, sound, or smell of that woman for forty years now!—even when I *laid* her!—regular as a piston. . . . Pretend to love that son of a bitch of a Gooper and his wife Mae and those five same screechers out there like parrots in a jungle? Jesus! Can't stand to look at 'em! Church!—it bores the Bejesus out of me but I go!—I go an' sit there and listen to the fool preacher! Clubs!—Elks! Masons! Rotary!—*crap*!

[*A spasm of pain makes him clutch his belly. He sinks into a chair and his voice is softer and hoarser.*]

You I *do* like for some reason, did always have some kind of real feeling for—affection—respect—yes, always. . . . You and being a success as a planter is all I ever had any devotion to in my whole life!—and that's the truth. . . . I don't know why, but it is! *I've* lived with mendacity!—Why can't *you* live with it? Hell, you *got* to live with it, there's nothing *else* to *live* with except mendacity, is there?

BRICK:

Yes, sir. Yes, sir there is something else that you can live with!

BIG DADDY:

What?

BRICK [*lifting his glass*]:

This!—Liquor. . . .

BIG DADDY:
That's not living, that's dodging away from life.

BRICK:
I want to dodge away from it.

BIG DADDY:
Then why don't you kill yourself, man?

BRICK:
I like to drink. . . .

BIG DADDY:
Oh, God, I can't talk to you. . . .

BRICK:
I'm sorry, Big Daddy.

BIG DADDY:
Not as sorry as I am. I'll tell you something. A little
while back when I thought my number was up—
   [*This speech should have torrential pace and fury.*]
—before I found out it was just this—spastic—colon, I
thought about you. Should I or should I not, if the jig
was up, give you this place when I go—since I hate
Gooper an' Mae an' know that they hate me, and since
all five same monkeys are little Maes an' Goopers.—
And I thought, No!—Then I thought, Yes!—I couldn't
make up my mind. I hate Gooper and his five same
monkeys and that bitch Mae! Why should I turn over
twenty-eight thousand acres of the richest land this side
of the valley Nile to not my kind?—But why in hell, on
the other hand, Brick—should I subsidize a goddam fool
on the bottle?—Liked or not liked, well, maybe even—
loved!—Why should I do that?—Subsidize worthless behavior? Rot? Corruption?

BRICK [*smiling*]:
I understand.

BIG DADDY:
Well, if you do, you're smarter than I am, God damn it,
because I don't understand. And this I will tell you
frankly. I didn't make up my mind at all on that question

and still to this day I ain't made out no will!—Well, now
I don't *have* to. The pressure is gone. I can just wait and
see if you pull yourself together or if you don't.

BRICK:
That's right, Big Daddy.

BIG DADDY:
You sound like you thought I was kidding.

BRICK [*rising*]:
No, sir, I know you're not kidding.

BIG DADDY:
But you don't care—?

BRICK [*hobbling toward the gallery door*]:
No, sir, I don't care. . . .
Now how about taking a look at your birthday fireworks
and getting some of that cool breeze off the river?

> [*He stands in the gallery doorway as the night sky
> turns pink and green and gold with successive flashes
> of light.*]

BIG DADDY:
WAIT!—Brick. . . .

> [*His voice drops. Suddenly there is something shy,
> almost tender, in his restraining gesture.*]

Don't let's—leave it like this, like them other talks we've
had, we've always—talked around things, we've—just
talked around things for some rutten reason. I don't
know what, it's always like something was left not spoken, something avoided because neither of us was honest
enough with the—other. . . .

BRICK:
I never lied to you, Big Daddy.

BIG DADDY:
Did I ever to *you?*

BRICK:
No, sir. . . .

BIG DADDY:
Then there is at least two people that never lied to each other.

BRICK:
But we've never *talked* to each other.

BIG DADDY:
We can *now*.

BRICK:
Big Daddy, there don't seem to be anything much to say.

BIG DADDY:
You say that you drink to kill your disgust with lying.

BRICK:
You said to give you a reason.

BIG DADDY:
Is liquor the only thing that'll kill this disgust?

BRICK:
Now. Yes.

BIG DADDY:
But not once, huh?

BRICK:
Not when I was still young an' believing. A drinking man's someone who wants to forget he isn't still young an' believing.

BIG DADDY:
Believing what?

BRICK:
Believing. . . .

BIG DADDY:
Believing *what*?

BRICK [*stubbornly evasive*]:
Believing. . . .

BIG DADDY:
I don't know what the hell you mean by believing and I don't think you know what you mean by believing, but

if you still got sports in your blood, go back to sports announcing and—

BRICK:
Sit in a glass box watching games I can't play? Describing what I can't do while players do it? Sweating out their disgust and confusion in contests I'm not fit for? Drinkin' a Coke, half bourbon, so I can stand it? That's no goddam good anymore, no help—time just outran me, Big Daddy—got there first . . .

BIG DADDY:
I think you're passing the buck.

BRICK:
You know many drinkin' men?

BIG DADDY [*with a slight, charming smile*]:
I have known a fair number of that species.

BRICK:
Could any of them tell you why he drank?

BIG DADDY:
Yep, you're passin' the buck to things like time and disgust with "mendacity" and—crap!—if you got to use that kind of language about a thing, it's ninety-proof bull, and I'm not buying any.

BRICK:
I had to give you a reason to get a drink!

BIG DADDY:
You started drinkin' when your friend Skipper died.

[*Silence for five beats. Then Brick makes a startled movement, reaching for his crutch.*]

BRICK:
What are you suggesting?

BIG DADDY:
I'm suggesting nothing.

[*The shuffle and clop of Brick's rapid hobble away from his father's steady, grave attention.*]

—But Gooper an' Mae suggested that there was something not right exactly in your—

BRICK [*stopping short downstage as if backed to a wall*]: "Not right"?

BIG DADDY:
Not, well, exactly *normal* in your friendship with—

BRICK:
They suggested that, too? I thought that was Maggie's suggestion.

> [*Brick's detachment is at last broken through. His heart is accelerated; his forehead sweat-beaded; his breath becomes more rapid and his voice hoarse. The thing they're discussing, timidly and painfully on the side of Big Daddy, fiercely, violently on Brick's side, is the inadmissible thing that Skipper died to disavow between them. The fact that if it existed it had to be disavowed to "keep face" in the world they lived in, may be at the heart of the "mendacity" that Brick drinks to kill his disgust with. It may be the root of his collapse. Or maybe it is only a single manifestation of it, not even the most important. The bird that I hope to catch in the net of this play is not the solution of one man's psychological problem. I'm trying to catch the true quality of experience in a group of people, that cloudy, flickering, evanescent— fiercely charged!—interplay of live human beings in the thundercloud of a common crisis. Some mystery should be left in the revelation of character in a play, just as a great deal of mystery is always left in the revelation of character in life, even in one's own character to himself. This does not absolve the playwright of his duty to observe and probe as clearly and deeply as he legitimately can: but it should steer him away from "pat" conclusions, facile definitions which make a play just a play, not a snare for the truth of human experience.*
> [*The following scene should be played with great concentration, with most of the power leashed but palpable in what is left unspoken.*]

Who else's suggestion is it, is it *yours?* How many others
thought that Skipper and I were—

BIG DADDY [*gently*]:
Now, hold on, hold on a minute, son.—I knocked around
in my time.

BRICK:
What's that got to do with—

BIG DADDY:
I said 'Hold on!'—I bummed, I bummed this country till
I was—

BRICK:
Whose suggestion, who else's suggestion is it?

BIG DADDY:
Slept in hobo jungles and railroad Y's and flophouses in
all cities before I—

BRICK:
Oh, *you* think so, too, you call me your son and a queer.
Oh! Maybe that's why you put Maggie and me in this
room that was Jack Straw's and Peter Ochello's, in
which that pair of old sisters slept in a double bed where
both of 'em died!

BIG DADDY:
Now just don't go throwing rocks at—

> [*Suddenly Reverend Tooker appears in the gallery
> doors, his head slightly, playfully, fatuously cocked,
> with a practiced clergyman's smile, sincere as a bird-
> call blown on a hunter's whistle, the living embodi-
> ment of the pious, conventional lie.*
> [*Big Daddy gasps a little at this perfectly timed, but
> incongruous, apparition.*]

—What're you lookin' for, Preacher?

REVEREND TOOKER:
The gentleman's lavatory, ha ha!—heh, heh . . .

BIG DADDY [*with strained courtesy*]:
—Go back out and walk down to the other end of the
gallery, Reverend Tooker, and use the bathroom con-

nected with my bedroom, and if you can't find it, ask them where it is!

REVEREND TOOKER:
Ah, thanks.

[*He goes out with a deprecatory chuckle.*]

BIG DADDY:
It's hard to talk in this place . . .

BRICK:
Son of a—!

BIG DADDY [*leaving a lot unspoken*]:
—I seen all things and understood a lot of them, till 1910. Christ, the year that—I had worn my shoes through, hocked my—I hopped off a yellow dog freight car half a mile down the road, slept in a wagon of cotton outside the gin—Jack Straw an' Peter Ochello took me in. Hired me to manage this place which grew into this one.—When Jack Straw died—why, old Peter Ochello quit eatin' like a dog does when its master's dead, and died, too!

BRICK:
Christ!

BIG DADDY:
I'm just saying I understand such—

BRICK [*violently*]:
Skipper is dead. I have not quit eating!

BIG DADDY:
No, but you started drinking.

[*Brick wheels on his crutch and hurls his glass across the room shouting.*]

BRICK:
YOU THINK SO, TOO?

BIG DADDY:
Shhh!

[*Footsteps run on the gallery. There are women's calls.*

[*Big Daddy goes toward the door.*]
Go way!—Just broke a glass. . . .

[*Brick is transformed, as if a quiet mountain blew suddenly up in volcanic flame.*]

BRICK:
You think so, too? You think so, too? You think me an' Skipper did, did, did!—*sodomy!*—together?

BIG DADDY:
Hold—!

BRICK:
That what you—

BIG DADDY:
—*ON*—a minute!

BRICK:
You think we did dirty things between us, Skipper an'—

BIG DADDY:
Why are you shouting like that? Why are you—

BRICK:
—Me, is that what you think of Skipper, is that—

BIG DADDY:
—so excited? I don't think nothing. I don't know nothing. I'm simply telling you what—

BRICK:
You think that Skipper and me were a pair of dirty old men?

BIG DADDY:
Now that's—

BRICK:
Straw? Ochello? A couple of—

BIG DADDY:
Now just—

BRICK:
—ducking sissies? Queers? Is that what you—

BIG DADDY:
Shhh.

BRICK:
—think?

[*He loses his balance and pitches to his knees without noticing the pain. He grabs the bed and drags himself up.*]

BIG DADDY:
Jesus!—Whew. . . . Grab my hand!

BRICK: ʼ
Naw, I don't want your hand. . . .

BIG DADDY:
Well, I want yours. Git up!

[*He draws him up, keeps an arm about him with concern and affection.*]

You broken out in a sweat! You're panting like you'd run a race with—

BRICK [*freeing himself from his father's hold*]:
Big Daddy, you shock me, Big Daddy, you, you—*shock* me! Talkin' so—

[*He turns away from his father.*]

—casually!—about a—thing like that . . .

—Don't you know how people *feel* about things like that? How, how *disgusted* they are by things like that? Why, at Ole Miss when it was discovered a pledge to our fraternity, Skipper's and mine, did a, *attempted* to do a, unnatural thing with—

We not only dropped him like a hot rock!—We told him to git off the campus, and he did, he got!—All the way to—

[*He halts, breathless.*]

BIG DADDY:
—Where?

BRICK:
—North Africa, last I heard!

BIG DADDY:
Well, I have come back from further away than that. I have just now returned from the other side of the moon, death's country, son, and I'm not easy to shock by anything here.

[*He comes downstage and faces out.*]

Always, anyhow, lived with too much space around me to be infected by ideas of other people. One thing you can grow on a big place more important than cotton!— is *tolerance!*—I grown it.

[*He returns toward Brick.*]

BRICK:
Why can't exceptional friendship, *real, real, deep, deep friendship!* between two men be respected as something clean and decent without being thought of as—

BIG DADDY:
It can, it is, for God's sake.

BRICK:
—*Fairies.* . . .

[*In his utterance of this word, we gauge the wide and profound reach of the conventional mores he got from the world that crowned him with early laurel.*]

BIG DADDY:
I told Mae an' Gooper—

BRICK:
Frig Mae and Gooper, frig all dirty lies and liars!—Skipper and me had a clean, true thing between us!—had a clean friendship, practically all our lives, till Maggie got the idea you're talking about. Normal? No!—It was too rare to be normal, any true thing between two people is too rare to be normal. Oh, once in a while he put his hand on my shoulder or I'd put mine on his, oh, maybe even, when we were touring the country in pro-football an' shared hotel-rooms we'd reach across the space between the two beds and shake hands to say goodnight, yeah, one or two times we—

BIG DADDY:
Brick, nobody thinks that that's not normal!

BRICK:
Well, they're mistaken, it was! It was a pure an' true
thing an' that's not normal.

[*They both stare straight at each other for a long
moment. The tension breaks and both turn away as
if tired.*]

BIG DADDY:
Yeah, it's—hard t'—talk. . . .

BRICK:
All right, then, let's—let it go. . . .

BIG DADDY:
Why did Skipper crack up? Why have you?

[*Brick looks back at his father again. He has already
decided, without knowing that he has made this deci-
sion, that he is going to tell his father that he is dying
of cancer. Only this could even the score between
them: one inadmissible thing in return for another.*]

BRICK [*ominously*]:
All right. You're asking for it, Big Daddy. We're finally
going to have that real true talk you wanted. It's too
late to stop it, now, we got to carry it through and cover
every subject.

[*He hobbles back to the liquor cabinet.*]
Uh-huh.

[*He opens the ice bucket and picks up the silver tongs
with slow admiration of their frosty brightness.*]

Maggie declares that Skipper and I went into pro-
football after we left "Ole Miss" because we were scared
to grow up . . .

[*He moves downstage with the shuffle and clop of a
cripple on a crutch. As Margaret did when her speech
became "recitative," he looks out into the house,
commanding its attention by his direct, concentrated
gaze—a broken, "tragically elegant" figure telling
simply as much as he knows of "the Truth":*]

—Wanted to—keep on tossing—those long, long!—high, high!—passes that—couldn't be intercepted except by time, the aerial attack that made us famous! And so we did, we did, we kept it up for one season, that aerial attack, we held it high!—Yeah, but—

—that summer, Maggie, she laid the law down to me, said, Now or never, and so I married Maggie. . . .

BIG DADDY:
How was Maggie in bed?

BRICK [*wryly*]:
Great! the greatest!

[*Big Daddy nods as if he thought so.*]

She went on the road that fall with the Dixie Stars. Oh, she made a great show of being the world's best sport. She wore a—wore a—tall bearskin cap! A shako, they call it, a dyed moleskin coat, a moleskin coat dyed red!—Cut up crazy! Rented hotel ballrooms for victory celebrations, wouldn't cancel them when it—turned out—defeat. . . . MAGGIE THE CAT! Ha ha!

[*Big Daddy nods.*]

—But Skipper, he had some fever which came back on him which doctors couldn't explain and I got that injury—turned out to be just a shadow on the X-ray plate—and a touch of bursitis. . . .
I lay in a hospital bed, watched our games on TV, saw Maggie on the bench next to Skipper when he was hauled out of a game for stumbles, fumbles!—Burned me up the way she hung on his arm!—Y'know, I think that Maggie had always felt sort of left out because she and me never got any closer together than two people just get in bed, which is not much closer than two cats on a—fence humping. . . .
So! She took this time to work on poor dumb Skipper. He was a less than average student at Ole Miss, you know that, don't you?!—Poured in his mind the dirty, false idea that what we were, him and me, was a frustrated case of that ole pair of sisters that lived in this room, Jack Straw and Peter Ochello!—He, poor Skipper, went to bed with Maggie to prove it wasn't true, and

when it didn't work out, he thought it *was* true!—
Skipper broke in two like a rotten stick—nobody ever
turned so fast to a lush—or died of it so quick. . . .
—Now are you satisfied?

[*Big Daddy has listened to this story, dividing the
grain from the chaff. Now he looks at his son.*]

BIG DADDY:
Are *you* satisfied?

BRICK:
With what?

BIG DADDY:
That half-ass story!

BRICK:
What's half-ass about it?

BIG DADDY:
Something's left out of that story. What did you leave
out?

[*The phone has started ringing in the hall. As if it
reminded him of something, Brick glances suddenly
toward the sound and says:*]

BRICK:
Yes!—I left out a long-distance call which I had from
Skipper, in which he made a drunken confession to me
and on which I hung up!—last time we spoke to each
other in our lives. . . .

[*Muted ring stops as someone answers phone in a
soft, indistinct voice in hall.*]

BIG DADDY:
You hung up?

BRICK:
Hung up. Jesus! Well—

BIG DADDY:
Anyhow now!—we have tracked down the lie with which
you're disgusted and which you are drinking to kill your
disgust with, Brick. You been passing the buck. This
disgust with mendacity is disgust with yourself.

You!—dug the grave of your friend and kicked him in it!—before you'd face truth with him!

BRICK:
His truth, not *mine!*

BIG DADDY:
His truth, okay! But you wouldn't face it with him!

BRICK:
Who *can* face truth? Can *you?*

BIG DADDY:
Now don't start passin' the rotten buck again, boy!

BRICK:
How about these birthday congratulations, these many, many happy returns of the day, when ev'rybody but you knows there won't be any!

> [*Whoever has answered the hall phone lets out a high, shrill laugh; the voice becomes audible saying: "no, no, you got it all wrong! Upside down! Are you crazy?"*
> [*Brick suddenly catches his breath as he realizes that he has made a shocking disclosure. He hobbles a few paces, then freezes, and without looking at his father's shocked face, says:*]

Let's, let's—go out, now, and—

> [*Big Daddy moves suddenly forward and grabs hold of the boy's crutch like it was a weapon for which they were fighting for possession.*]

BIG DADDY:
Oh, no, no! No one's going out. What did you start to say?

BRICK:
I don't remember.

BIG DADDY:
"Many happy returns when they know there won't be any"?

BRICK:

Aw, hell, Big Daddy, forget it. Come on out on the gallery and look at the fireworks they're shooting off for your birthday. . . .

BIG DADDY:

First you finish that remark you were makin' before you cut off. "Many happy returns when they know there won't be any"?—Ain't that what you just said?

BRICK:

Look, now. I can get around without that crutch if I have to but it would be a lot easier on the furniture an' glassware if I didn' have to go swinging along like Tarzan of th'—

BIG DADDY:

FINISH! WHAT YOU WAS SAYIN'!

[*An eerie green glow shows in sky behind him.*]

BRICK [*sucking the ice in his glass, speech becoming thick*]:
Leave th' place to Gooper and Mae an' their five little same little monkeys. All I want is—

BIG DADDY:

"LEAVE TH' PLACE," did you say?

BRICK [*vaguely*]:

All twenty-eight thousand acres of the richest land this side of the valley Nile.

BIG DADDY:

Who said I was "leaving the place" to Gooper or anybody? This is my sixty-fifth birthday! I got fifteen years or twenty years left in me! I'll outlive *you!* I'll bury you an' have to pay for your coffin!

BRICK:

Sure. Many happy returns. Now let's go watch the fireworks, come on, let's—

BIG DADDY:

Lying, have they been lying? About the report from

th'—clinic? Did they, did they—find something?—
Cancer. Maybe?

BRICK:
Mendacity is a system that we live in. Liquor is one way
out an' death's the other. . . .

> [*He takes the crutch from Big Daddy's loose grip
> and swings out on the gallery leaving the doors open.*
> [*A song, "Pick a Bale of Cotton," is heard.*]

MAE [*appearing in door*]:
Oh, Big Daddy, the field-hands are singin' fo' you!

BIG DADDY [*shouting hoarsely*]:
BRICK! BRICK!

MAE:
He's outside drinkin', Big Daddy.

BIG DADDY:
BRICK!

> [*Mae retreats, awed by the passion of his voice. Chil-
> dren call Brick in tones mocking Big Daddy. His
> face crumbles like broken yellow plaster about to fall
> into dust.*
> [*There is a glow in the sky. Brick swings back
> through the doors, slowly, gravely, quite soberly.*]

BRICK:
I'm sorry, Big Daddy. My head don't work any more
and it's hard for me to understand how anybody could
care if he lived or died or was dying or cared about
anything but whether or not there was liquor left in the
bottle and so I said what I said without thinking. In
some ways I'm no better than the others, in some ways
worse because I'm less alive. Maybe it's being alive that
makes them lie, and being almost *not* alive makes me sort
of accidentally truthful—I don't know but—anyway—
we've been friends . . .
—And being friends is telling each other the truth. . . .

> [*There is a pause.*]

You told *me!* I told *you!*

[*A child rushes into the room and grabs a fistful of firecrackers and runs out again.*]

CHILD [*screaming*]:
Bang, bang, bang, bang bang, bang, bang, bang, bang!

BIG DADDY [*slowly and passionately*]:
CHRIST—DAMN—ALL—LYING SONS OF—LYING BITCHES!

[*He straightens at last and crosses to the inside door. At the door he turns and looks back as if he had some desperate question he couldn't put into words. Then he nods reflectively and says in a hoarse voice:*]

Yes, all liars, all liars, all lying dying liars!

[*This is said slowly, slowly, with a fierce revulsion. He goes on out.*]

—Lying! Dying! Liars!

[*His voice dies out. There is the sound of a child being slapped. It rushes, hideously bawling, through room and out the hall door.*
[*Brick remains motionless as the lights dim out and the curtain falls.*]

CURTAIN

ACT THREE

There is no lapse of time. Mae enters with Reverend Tooker.

MAE:
Where is Big Daddy! Big Daddy?

BIG MAMA [*entering*]:
Too much smell of burnt fireworks makes me feel a little bit sick at my stomach.—Where is Big Daddy?

MAE:
That's what I want to know, where has Big Daddy gone?

BIG MAMA:
He must have turned in, I reckon he went to baid. . . .
[*Gooper enters.*]

GOOPER:
Where is Big Daddy?

MAE:
We don't know where he is!

BIG MAMA:
I reckon he's gone to baid.

GOOPER:
Well, then, now we can talk.

BIG MAMA:
What *is* this talk, *what* talk?
[*Margaret appears on gallery, talking to Dr. Baugh.*]

MARGARET [*musically*]:
My family freed their slaves ten years before abolition, my great-great-grandfather gave his slaves their freedom five years before the war between the States started!

MAE:
Oh, for God's sake! Maggie's climbed back up in her family tree!

MARGARET [*sweetly*]:
What, Mae?—Oh, where's Big Daddy?!

[*The pace must be very quick. Great Southern animation.*]

BIG MAMA [*addressing them all*]:
I think Big Daddy was just worn out. He loves his family, he loves to have them around him, but it's a strain on his nerves. He wasn't himself tonight, Big Daddy wasn't himself, I could tell he was all worked up.

REVEREND TOOKER:
I think he's remarkable.

BIG MAMA:
Yaisss! Just remarkable. Did you all notice the food he ate at that table? Did you all notice the supper he put away? Why, he ate like a hawss!

GOOPER:
I hope he doesn't regret it.

BIG MAMA:
Why, that man—ate a huge piece of cawn-bread with molasses on it! Helped himself twice to hoppin' john.

MARGARET:
Big Daddy loves hoppin' john.—We had a real country dinner.

BIG MAMA [*overlapping Margaret*]:
Yais, he simply adores it! An' candied yams? That man put away enough food at that table to stuff a nigger *field*-hand!

GOOPER [*with grim relish*]:
I hope he don't have to pay for it later on. . . .

BIG MAMA [*fiercely*]:
What's *that*, Gooper?

MAE:
Gooper says he hopes Big Daddy doesn't suffer tonight.

BIG MAMA:
Oh, shoot, Gooper says, Gooper says! Why should Big Daddy suffer for satisfying a normal appetite? There's nothin' wrong with that man but nerves, he's sound as a dollar! And now he knows he is an' that's why he ate such a supper. He had a big load off his mind, knowin' he wasn't doomed t'—what he thought he was doomed to. . . .

MARGARET [*sadly and sweetly*]:
Bless his old sweet soul. . . .

BIG MAMA [*vaguely*]:
Yais, bless his heart, wher's Brick?

MAE:
Outside.

GOOPER:
—Drinkin' . . .

BIG MAMA:
I know he's drinkin'. You all don't have to keep tellin' *me* Brick is drinkin'. Cain't I see he's drinkin' without you continually tellin' me that boy's drinkin'?

MARGARET:
Good for you, Big Mama!
    [*She applauds.*]

BIG MAMA:
Other people *drink* and *have* drunk an' will *drink,* as long as they make that stuff an' put it in bottles.

MARGARET:
That's the truth. I never trusted a man that didn't drink.

MAE:
Gooper never drinks. Don't you trust Gooper?

MARGARET:
Why, Gooper don't you drink? If I'd known you didn't drink, I wouldn't of made that remark—

BIG MAMA:
Brick?

MARGARET:
—at least not in your presence.

[*She laughs sweetly.*]

BIG MAMA:
Brick!

MARGARET:
He's still on the gall'ry. I'll go bring him in so we can talk.

BIG MAMA [*worriedly*]:
I don't know what this mysterious family conference is about.

[*Awkward silence. Big Mama looks from face to face, then belches slightly and mutters, "Excuse me. . . ." She opens an ornamental fan suspended about her throat, a black lace fan to go with her black lace gown, and fans her wilting corsage, sniffing nervously and looking from face to face in the uncomfortable silence as Margaret calls "Brick?" and Brick sings to the moon on the gallery.*]

I don't know what's wrong here, you all have such long faces! Open that door on the hall and let some air circulate through here, will you please, Gooper?

MAE:
I think we'd better leave that door closed, Big Mama, till after the talk.

BIG MAMA:
Reveren' Tooker, will *you* please open that door?!

REVEREND TOOKER:
I sure will, Big Mama.

MAE:
I just didn't think we ought t' take any chance of Big Daddy hearin' a word of this discussion.

BIG MAMA:
I swan! Nothing's going to be said in Big Daddy's house that he cain't hear if he wants to!

GOOPER:
Well, Big Mama, it's—

[*Mae gives him a quick, hard poke to shut him up. He glares at her fiercely as she circles before him like a burlesque ballerina, raising her skinny bare arms over her head, jangling her bracelets, exclaiming:*]

MAE:
A breeze! A breeze!

REVEREND TOOKER:
I think this house is the coolest house in the Delta.— Did you all know that Halsey Banks' widow put air-conditioning units in the church and rectory at Friar's Point in memory of Halsey?

[*General conversation has resumed; everybody is chatting so that the stage sounds like a big bird-cage.*]

GOOPER:
Too bad nobody cools your church off for you. I bet you sweat in that pulpit these hot Sundays, Reverend Tooker.

REVEREND TOOKER:
Yes, my vestments are drenched.

MAE [*at the same time to Dr. Baugh*]:
You reckon those vitamin B_{12} injections are what they're cracked up t' be, Doc Baugh?

DOCTOR BAUGH:
Well, if you want to be stuck with something I guess they're as good to be stuck with as anything else.

BIG MAMA [*at gallery door*]:
Maggie, Maggie, aren't you comin' with Brick?

MAE [*suddenly and loudly, creating a silence*]:
I have a strange feeling, I have a peculiar feeling!

BIG MAMA [*turning from gallery*]:
What feeling?

MAE:
That Brick said somethin' he shouldn't of said t' Big
Daddy.

BIG MAMA:
Now what on earth could Brick of said t' Big Daddy
that he shouldn't say?

GOOPER:
Big Mama, there's somethin'—

MAE:
NOW, WAIT!

> [*She rushes up to Big Mama and gives her a quick
> hug and kiss. Big Mama pushes her impatiently off
> as the Reverend Tooker's voice rises serenely in a
> little pocket of silence:*]

REVEREND TOOKER:
Yes, last Sunday the gold in my chasuble faded into
th' purple. . . .

GOOPER:
Reveren', you must of been preachin' hell's fire last
Sunday!

> [*He guffaws at this witticism but the Reverend is not
> sincerely amused. At the same time Big Mama has
> crossed over to Dr. Baugh and is saying to him:*]

BIG MAMA [*her breathless voice rising high-pitched above
the others*]:
In my day they had what they call the Keeley cure for
heavy drinkers. But now I understand they just take
some kind of tablets, they call them "Annie Bust" tablets. But *Brick* don't need to take *nothin'*.

> [*Brick appears in gallery doors with Margaret behind
> him. Unaware of his presence behind her, Big
> Mama says:*]

That boy is just broken up over Skipper's death. You
know how poor Skipper died. They gave him a big, big

dose of that sodium amytal stuff at his home and then
they called the ambulance and give him another big, big
dose of it at the hospital and that and all of the alcohol
in his system fo' months an' months an' months just
proved too much for his heart. . . . I'm scared of needles!
I'm more scared of a needle than the knife. . . . I think
more people have been needled out of this world than—

[*She stops short and wheels about.*]

OH!—here's Brick! My precious baby—

[*She turns upon Brick with short, fat arms extended,
at the same time uttering a loud, short sob, which is
both comic and touching.*

[*Brick smiles and bows slightly, making a burlesque
gesture of gallantry for Maggie to pass before him
into the room. Then he hobbles on his crutch directly
to the liquor cabinet and there is absolute silence,
with everybody looking at Brick as everybody has
always looked at Brick when he spoke or moved or
appeared. One by one he drops ice cubes in his glass,
then suddenly, but not quickly, looks back over his
shoulder with a wry, charming smile, and says:*]

BRICK:
I'm sorry! Anyone else?

BIG MAMA [*sadly*]:
No, son. I *wish* you wouldn't!

BRICK:
I wish I didn't have to, Big Mama, but I'm still waiting
for that click in my head which makes it all smooth out!

BIG MAMA:
Aw, Brick, you—BREAK MY HEART!

MARGARET [*at the same time*]:
Brick, go sit with Big Mama!

BIG MAMA:
I just cain't *staiiiiiiiii-nnnnnd*—it. . . .

[*She sobs.*]

MAE:
Now that we're all assembled—

GOOPER:
We kin talk. . . .

BIG MAMA:
Breaks my heart. . . .

MARGARET:
Sit with Big Mama, Brick, and hold her hand.

[*Big Mama sniffs very loudly three times, almost like three drum beats in the pocket of silence.*]

BRICK:
You do that, Maggie. I'm a restless cripple. I got to stay on my crutch.

[*Brick hobbles to the gallery door; leans there as if waiting.*
[*Mae sits beside Big Mama, while Gooper moves in front and sits on the end of the couch, facing her. Reverend Tooker moves nervously into the space between them; on the other side, Dr. Baugh stands looking at nothing in particular and lights a cigar. Margaret turns away.*]

BIG MAMA:
Why're you all *surroundin'* me—like this? Why're you all starin' at me like this an' makin' signs at each other?

[*Reverend Tooker steps back startled.*]

MAE:
Calm yourself, Big Mama.

BIG MAMA:
Calm you'self, *you'self,* Sister Woman. How could I calm myself with everyone starin' at me as if big drops of blood had broken out on m'face? What's this all about, Annh! What?

[*Gooper coughs and takes a center position.*]

GOOPER:
Now, Doc Baugh.

MAE:
Doc Baugh?

BRICK [*suddenly*]:
SHHH!—

> [*Then he grins and chuckles and shakes his head
> regretfully.*]

—Naw!—that wasn't th' click.

GOOPER:
Brick, shut up or stay out there on the gallery with your
liquor! We got to talk about a serious matter. Big Mama
wants to know the complete truth about the report we
got today from the Ochsner Clinic.

MAE [*eagerly*]:
—on Big Daddy's condition!

GOOPER:
Yais, on Big Daddy's condition, we got to face it.

DOCTOR BAUGH:
Well. . . .

BIG MAMA [*terrified, rising*]:
Is there? Something? Something that I? Don't—Know?

> [*In these few words, this startled, very soft, question,
> Big Mama reviews the history of her forty-five years
> with Big Daddy, her great, almost embarrassingly
> true-hearted and simple-minded devotion to Big
> Daddy, who must have had something Brick has,
> who made himself loved so much by the "simple expe-
> dient" of not loving enough to disturb his charming
> detachment, also once coupled, like Brick's, with vir-
> ile beauty.*
> [*Big Mama has a dignity at this moment: she almost
> stops being fat.*]

DOCTOR BAUGH [*after a pause, uncomfortably*]:
Yes?—Well—

BIG MAMA:
I!!!—want to—knowwwwwww. . . .

> [*Immediately she thrusts her fist to her mouth as if
> to deny that statement.
> [*Then, for some curious reason, she snatches the*

*withered corsage from her breast and hurls it on the
floor and steps on it with her short, fat feet.*]

—*Somebody must be lyin'!—I want to know!*

MAE:
Sit down, Big Mama, sit down on this sofa.

MARGARET [*quickly*]:
Brick, go sit with Big Mama.

BIG MAMA:
What is it, what is it?

DOCTOR BAUGH:
I never have seen a more thorough examination than
Big Daddy Pollitt was given in all my experience with
the Ochsner Clinic.

GOOPER:
It's one of the best in the country.

MAE:
It's *THE* best in the country—bar *none!*

   [*For some reason she gives Gooper a violent poke
   as she goes past him. He slaps at her hand without
   removing his eyes from his mother's face.*]

DOCTOR BAUGH:
Of course they were ninety-nine and nine-tenths percent
sure before they even started.

BIG MAMA:
Sure of what, sure of what, sure of—*what?—what!*

   [*She catches her breath in a startled sob. Mae kisses
   her quickly. She thrusts Mae fiercely away from her,
   staring at the doctor.*]

MAE:
Mommy, be a brave girl!

BRICK [*in the doorway, softly*]:
*By the light, by the light,
Of the sil-ve-ry mo-ooo-n . . .*

GOOPER:
Shut up!—Brick.

BRICK:
—Sorry. . . .

[*He wanders out on the gallery.*]

DOCTOR BAUGH:
But now, you see, Big Mama, they cut a piece off this growth, a specimen of the tissue and—

BIG MAMA:
Growth? You told Big Daddy—

DOCTOR BAUGH:
Now wait.

BIG MAMA [*fiercely*]:
You told me and Big Daddy there wasn't a thing wrong with him but—

MAE:
Big Mama, they always—

GOOPER:
Let Doc Baugh talk, will yuh?

BIG MAMA:
—little spastic condition of—

[*Her breath gives out in a sob.*]

DOCTOR BAUGH:
Yes, that's what we told Big Daddy. But we had this bit of tissue run through the laboratory and I'm sorry to say the test was positive on it. It's—well—malignant. . . .

[*Pause.*]

BIG MAMA:
—Cancer?! Cancer?!

[*Dr. Baugh nods gravely.*
[*Big Mama gives a long gasping cry.*]

MAE and GOOPER:
Now, now, now, Big Mama, you had to know. . . .

BIG MAMA:
WHY DIDN'T THEY CUT IT OUT OF HIM?
HANH? HANH?

DOCTOR BAUGH:
Involved too much, Big Mama, too many organs
affected.

MAE:
Big Mama, the liver's affected and so's the kidneys,
both! It's gone way past what they call a—

GOOPER:
A surgical risk.

MAE:
—Uh-huh. . . .
   [*Big Mama draws a breath like a dying gasp.*]

REVEREND TOOKER:
Tch, tch, tch, tch, tch!

DOCTOR BAUGH:
Yes, it's gone past the knife.

MAE:
That's why he's turned yellow, Mommy!

BIG MAMA:
Git away from me, git away from me, Mae!
   [*She rises abruptly.*]
I want Brick! Where's Brick? Where is my only son?

MAE:
Mama! Did she say "*only* son"?

GOOPER:
What does that make *me?*

MAE:
A sober responsible man with five precious children!—
Six!

BIG MAMA:
I want Brick to tell me! Brick! Brick!

MARGARET [*rising from her reflections in a corner*]:
Brick was so upset he went back out.

BIG MAMA:
Brick!

MARGARET:
Mama, let *me* tell you!

BIG MAMA:
No, no, leave me alone, you're not my blood!

GOOPER:
Mama, I'm your son! Listen to *me!*

MAE:
Gooper's your son, he's your first-born!

BIG MAMA:
Gooper never liked Daddy.

MAE [*as if terribly shocked*]:
That's not TRUE!

  [*There is a pause. The minister coughs and rises.*]

REVEREND TOOKER [*to Mae*]:
I think I'd better slip away at this point.

MAE [*sweetly and sadly*]:
Yes, Doctor Tooker, you go.

REVEREND TOOKER [*discreetly*]:
Goodnight, goodnight, everybody, and God bless you
all . . . on this place. . . .

  [*He slips out.*]

DOCTOR BAUGH:
That man is a good man but lacking in tact. Talking
about people giving memorial windows—if he mentioned one memorial window, he must have spoke of a
dozen, and saying how awful it was when somebody died
intestate, the legal wrangles, and so forth.

  [*Mae coughs, and points at Big Mama.*]
Well, Big Mama. . . .

  [*He sighs.*]

BIG MAMA:
It's all a mistake, I know it's just a bad dream.

DOCTOR BAUGH:
We're gonna keep Big Daddy as comfortable as we can.

BIG MAMA:
Yes, it's just a bad dream, that's all it is, it's just an awful dream.

GOOPER:
In my opinion Big Daddy is having some pain but won't admit that he has it.

BIG MAMA:
Just a dream, a bad dream.

DOCTOR BAUGH:
That's what lots of them do, they think if they don't admit they're having the pain they can sort of escape the fact of it.

GOOPER [*with relish*]:
Yes, they get sly about it, they get real sly about it.

MAE:
Gooper and I think—

GOOPER:
Shut up, Mae!—Big Daddy ought to be started on morphine.

BIG MAMA:
Nobody's going to give Big Daddy morphine.

DOCTOR BAUGH:
Now, Big Mama, when that pain strikes it's going to strike mighty hard and Big Daddy's going to need the needle to bear it.

BIG MAMA:
I tell you, nobody's going to give him morphine.

MAE:
Big Mama, you don't want to see Big Daddy suffer, you know you—

[*Gooper standing beside her gives her a savage poke.*]

DOCTOR BAUGH [*placing a package on the table*]:
I'm leaving this stuff here, so if there's a sudden attack you all won't have to send out for it.

MAE:
I know how to give a hypo.

GOOPER:
Mae took a course in nursing during the war.

MARGARET:
Somehow I don't think Big Daddy would want Mae to give him a hypo.

MAE:
You think he'd want *you* to do it?
[*Dr. Baugh rises.*]

GOOPER:
Doctor Baugh is goin'.

DOCTOR BAUGH:
Yes, I got to be goin'. Well, keep your chin up, Big Mama.

GOOPER [*with jocularity*]:
She's gonna keep *both* chins up, aren't you, Big Mama?
[*Big Mama sobs.*]
Now stop that, Big Mama.

MAE:
Sit down with me, Big Mama.

GOOPER [*at door with Dr. Baugh*]:
Well, Doc, we sure do appreciate all you done. I'm telling you, we're surely obligated to you for—
[*Dr. Baugh has gone out without a glance at him.*]
—I guess that doctor has got a lot on his mind but it wouldn't hurt him to act a little more human. . . .
[*Big Mama sobs.*]
Now be a brave girl, Mommy.

BIG MAMA:
It's not true, I know that it's just not true!

GOOPER:
Mama, those tests are infallible!

BIG MAMA:
Why are you so determined to see your father daid?

MAE:
Big Mama!

MARGARET [*gently*]:
I know what Big Mama means.

MAE [*fiercely*]:
Oh, do you?

MARGARET [*quietly and very sadly*]:
Yes, I think I do.

MAE:
For a newcomer in the family you sure do show a lot of understanding.

MARGARET:
Understanding is needed on this place.

MAE:
I guess you must have needed a lot of it in your family, Maggie, with your father's liquor problem and now you've got Brick with his!

MARGARET:
Brick does not have a liquor problem at all. Brick is devoted to Big Daddy. This thing is a terrible strain on him.

BIG MAMA:
Brick is Big Daddy's boy, but he drinks too much and it worries me and Big Daddy, and, Margaret, you've got to cooperate with us, you've got to cooperate with Big Daddy and me in getting Brick straightened out. Because it will break Big Daddy's heart if Brick don't pull himself together and take hold of things.

MAE:
Take hold of *what* things, Big Mama?

BIG MAMA:
The place.

> [*There is a quick violent look between Mae and Gooper.*]

GOOPER:
Big Mama, you've had a shock.

MAE:
Yais, we've all had a shock, but. . . .

GOOPER:
Let's be realistic—

MAE:
—Big Daddy would never, would *never,* be foolish enough to—

GOOPER:
—put this place in irresponsible hands!

BIG MAMA:
Big Daddy ain't going to leave the place in anybody's hands; Big Daddy is *not* going to die. I want you to get that in your heads, all of you!

MAE:
Mommy, Mommy, Big Mama, we're just as hopeful an' optimistic as you are about Big Daddy's prospects, we have faith in *prayer*—but nevertheless there are certain matters that have to be discussed an' dealt with, because otherwise—

GOOPER:
Eventualities have to be considered and now's the time. . . . Mae, will you please get my briefcase out of our room?

MAE:
Yes, honey.

> [*She rises and goes out through the hall door.*]

GOOPER [standing over Big Mama]:
Now Big Mom. What you said just now was not at all
true and you know it. I've always loved Big Daddy in
my own quiet way. I never made a show of it, and I
know that Big Daddy has always been fond of me in a
quiet way, too, and he never made a show of it neither.

[Mae returns with Gooper's briefcase.]

MAE:
Here's your briefcase, Gooper, honey.

GOOPER [handing the briefcase back to her]:
Thank you. . . . Of cou'se, my relationship with Big
Daddy is different from Brick's.

MAE:
You're eight years older'n Brick an' always had t'carry
a bigger load of th' responsibilities than Brick ever had
t'carry. He never carried a thing in his life but a football
or a highball.

GOOPER:
Mae, will y' let me talk, please?

MAE:
Yes, honey.

GOOPER:
Now, a twenty-eight-thousand-acre plantation's a mighty
big thing t'run.

MAE:
Almost single-handed.

[Margaret has gone out onto the gallery, and can be
heard calling softly to Brick.]

BIG MAMA:
You never had to run this place! What are you talking
about? As if Big Daddy was dead and in his grave, you
had to run it? Why, you just helped him out with a few
business details and had your law practice at the same
time in Memphis!

MAE:
Oh, Mommy, Mommy, Big Mommy! Let's be fair! Why,

Gooper has given himself body and soul to keeping this place up for the past five years since Big Daddy's health started failing. Gooper won't say it, Gooper never thought of it as a duty, he just did it. And what did Brick do? Brick kept living in his past glory at college! Still a football player at twenty-seven!

MARGARET [*returning alone*]:
Who are you talking about, now? Brick? A football player? He isn't a football player and you know it. Brick is a sports announcer on TV and one of the best-known ones in the country!

MAE:
I'm talking about what he was.

MARGARET:
Well, I wish you would just stop talking about my husband.

GOOPER:
I've got a right to discuss my brother with other members of MY OWN family which don't include *you*. Why don't you go out there and drink with Brick?

MARGARET:
I've never seen such malice toward a brother.

GOOPER:
How about his for me? Why, he can't stand to be in the same room with me!

MARGARET:
This is a deliberate campaign of vilification for the most disgusting and sordid reason on earth, and I know what it is! It's *avarice, avarice, greed, greed!*

BIG MAMA:
Oh, I'll scream! I will scream in a moment unless this stops!

[*Gooper has stalked up to Margaret with clenched fists at his sides as if he would strike her. Mae distorts her face again into a hideous grimace behind Margaret's back.*]

MARGARET:
We only remain on the place because of Big Mom and Big Daddy. If it is true what they say about Big Daddy we are going to leave here just as soon as it's over. Not a moment later.

BIG MAMA [sobs]:
Margaret. Child. Come here. Sit next to Big Mama.

MARGARET:
Precious Mommy. I'm sorry, I'm sorry, I—!

> [She bends her long graceful neck to press her fore-head to Big Mama's bulging shoulder under its black chiffon.]

GOOPER:
How beautiful, how touching, this display of devotion!

MAE:
Do you know why she's childless? She's childless because that big beautiful athlete husband of hers won't go to bed with her!

GOOPER:
You jest won't let me do this in a nice way, will yah? Aw right—Mae and I have five kids with another one coming! I don't give a goddam if Big Daddy likes me or don't like me or did or never did or will or will never! I'm just appealing to a sense of common decency and fair play. I'll tell you the truth. I've resented Big Daddy's partiality to Brick ever since Brick was born, and the way I've been treated like I was just barely good enough to spit on and sometimes not even good enough for that. Big Daddy is dying of cancer, and it's spread all through him and it's attacked all his vital organs including the kidneys and right now he is sinking into uremia, and you all know what uremia is, it's poisoning of the whole system due to the failure of the body to eliminate its poisons.

MARGARET [to herself, downstage, hissingly]:
Poisons, poisons! Venomous thoughts and words! In hearts and minds!—That's poisons!

GOOPER [*overlapping her*]:
I am asking for a square deal, and I expect to get one.
But if I don't get one, if there's any peculiar shenanigans
going on around here behind my back, or before me,
well, I'm not a corporation lawyer for nothing, I know
how to protect my own interests. —*OH! A late arrival!*

[*Brick enters from the gallery with a tranquil, blurred
smile, carrying an empty glass with him.*]

MAE:
Behold the conquering hero comes!

GOOPER:
The fabulous Brick Pollitt! Remember him?—Who
could forget him!

MAE:
He looks like he's been injured in a game!

GOOPER:
Yep, I'm afraid you'll have to warm the bench at the
Sugar Bowl this year, Brick!

[*Mae laughs shrilly.*]

Or was it the Rose Bowl that he made that famous
run in?

MAE:
The punch bowl, honey. It was in the punch bowl, the
cut-glass punch bowl!

GOOPER:
Oh, that's right, I'm getting the bowls mixed up!

MARGARET:
Why don't you stop venting your malice and envy on a
sick boy?

BIG MAMA:
Now you two hush, I mean it, hush, all of you, hush!

GOOPER:
All right, Big Mama. A family crisis brings out the best
and the worst in every member of it.

MAE:
That's the truth.

MARGARET:
Amen!

BIG MAMA:
I said, hush! I won't tolerate any more catty talk in my house.

> [*Mae gives Gooper a sign indicating the briefcase.*
> [*Brick's smile has grown both brighter and vaguer. As he prepares a drink, he sings softly:*]

BRICK:
Show me the way to go home,
I'm tired and I wanta go to bed,
I had a little drink about an hour ago—

GOOPER [*at the same time*]:
Big Mama, you know it's necessary for me t'go back to Memphis in th' mornin' t'represent the Parker estate in a lawsuit.

> [*Mae sits on the bed and arranges papers she has taken from the briefcase.*]

BRICK [*continuing the song*]:
Wherever I may roam,
On land or sea or foam.

BIG MAMA:
Is it, Gooper?

MAE:
Yaiss.

GOOPER:
That's why I'm forced to—to bring up a problem that—

MAE:
Somethin' that's too important t' be put off!

GOOPER:
If Brick was sober, he ought to be in on this.

MARGARET:
Brick is present; we're here.

GOOPER:
Well, good. I will now give you this outline my partner, Tom Bullitt, an' me have drawn up—a sort of dummy—trusteeship.

MARGARET:
Oh, that's it! You'll be in charge an' dole out remittances, will you?

GOOPER:
This we did as soon as we got the report on Big Daddy from th' Ochsner Laboratories. We did this thing, I mean we drew up this dummy outline with the advice and assistance of the Chairman of the Boa'd of Directors of th' Southern Plantahs Bank and Trust Company in Memphis, C. C. Bellowes, a man who handles estates for all th' prominent fam'lies in West Tennessee and th' Delta.

BIG MAMA:
Gooper?

GOOPER [*crouching in front of Big Mama*]:
Now this is not—not final, or anything like it. This is just a preliminary outline. But it does provide a basis— a design—a—possible, fe isible—*plan!*

MARGARET:
Yes, I'll bet.

MAE:
It's a plan to protect the biggest estate in the Delta from irresponsibility an'—

BIG MAMA:
Now you listen to me, all of you, you listen here! They's not goin' to be any more catty talk in my house! And Gooper, you put that away before I grab it out of your hand and tear it right up! I don't know what the hell's in it, and I don't want to know what the hell's in it. I'm talkin' in Big Daddy's language now; I'm his *wife,* not his *widow,* I'm still his *wife!* And I'm talkin' to you in his language an'—

GOOPER:
Big Mama, what I have here is—

MAE:
Gooper explained that it's just a plan. . . .

BIG MAMA:
I don't care what you got there. Just put it back where it came from, an' don't let me see it again, not even the outside of the envelope of it! Is that understood? Basis! Plan! Preliminary! Design! I say—what is it Big Daddy always says when he's disgusted?

BRICK [*from the bar*]:
Big Daddy says "crap" when he's disgusted.

BIG MAMA [*rising*]:
That's right—*CRAP!* I say *CRAP* too, like Big Daddy!

MAE:
Coarse language doesn't seem called for in this—

GOOPER:
Somethin' in me is *deeply outraged* by hearin' you talk like this.

BIG MAMA:
Nobody's goin' to take nothin'!—till Big Daddy lets go if it, and maybe, just possibly, not—not even then! No, not even then!

BRICK:
You can always hear me singin' this song,
Show me the way to go home.

BIG MAMA:
Tonight Brick looks like he used to look when he was a little boy, just like he did when he played wild games and used to come home all sweaty and pink-cheeked and sleepy, with his—red curls shining. . . .

> [*She comes over to him and runs her fat shaky hand through his hair. He draws aside as he does from all physical contact and continues the song in a whisper, opening the ice bucket and dropping in the ice cubes*

*one by one as if he were mixing some important
chemical formula.*]

Time goes by so fast. Nothin' can outrun it. Death commences too early—almost before you're half-acquainted
with life—you meet with the other. . . .

Oh, you know we just got to love each other an' stay
together, all of us, just as close as we can, especially now
that such a *black* thing has come and moved into this
place without invitation.

[*Awkwardly embracing Brick, she presses her head
to his shoulder.*

[*Gooper has been returning papers to Mae who has
restored them to briefcase with an air of severely
tried patience.*]

GOOPER:
Big Mama? Big Mama?

[*He stands behind her, tense with sibling envy.*]

BIG MAMA [*oblivious of Gooper*]:
Brick, you hear me, don't you?

MARGARET:
Brick hears you, Big Mama, he understands what you're
saying.

BIG MAMA:
Oh, Brick, son of Big Daddy! Big Daddy does so love
you! Y'know what would be his fondest dream come
true? If before he passed on, if Big Daddy has to pass
on, you gave him a child of yours, a grandson as much
like his son as his son is like Big Daddy!

MAE [*zipping briefcase shut: an incongruous sound*]:
Such a pity that Maggie an' Brick can't oblige!

MARGARET [*suddenly and quietly but forcefully*]:
Everybody listen.

[*She crosses to the center of the room, holding her
hands rigidly together.*]

MAE:
Listen to what, Maggie?

MARGARET:
I have an announcement to make.

GOOPER:
A sports announcement, Maggie?

MARGARET:
Brick and I are going to—*have a child!*

> [*Big Mama catches her breath in a loud gasp.*
> [*Pause. Big Mama rises.*]

BIG MAMA:
Maggie! Brick! This is too good to believe!

MAE:
That's right, too good to believe.

BIG MAMA:
Oh, my, my! This is Big Daddy's dream, his dream come
true! I'm going to tell him right now before he—

MARGARET:
We'll tell him in the morning. Don't disturb him now.

BIG MAMA:
I want to tell him before he goes to sleep, I'm going to
tell him his dream's come true this minute! And Brick!
A child will make you pull yourself together and quit
this drinking!

> [*She seizes the glass from his hand.*]

The responsibilities of a father will—

> [*Her face contorts and she makes an excited gesture;
> bursting into sobs, she rushes out, crying.*]

I'm going to tell Big Daddy right this minute!

> [*Her voice fades out down the hall.*
> [*Brick shrugs slightly and drops an ice cube into an-
> other glass. Margaret crosses quickly to his side, say-
> ing something under her breath, and she pours the
> liquor for him, staring up almost fiercely into his
> face.*]

BRICK [*coolly*]:
Thank you, Maggie, that's a nice big shot.

[*Mae has joined Gooper and she gives him a fierce poke, making a low hissing sound and a grimace of fury.*]

GOOPER [*pushing her aside*]:
Brick, could you possibly spare me one small shot of that liquor?

BRICK:
Why, help yourself, Gooper boy.

GOOPER:
I will.

MAE [*shrilly*]:
Of course we know that this is—

GOOPER:
Be still, Mae!

MAE:
I won't be still! I know she's made this up!

GOOPER:
Goddam it, I said to shut up!

MARGARET:
Gracious! I didn't know that my little announcement was going to provoke such a storm!

MAE:
That woman isn't *pregnant!*

GOOPER:
Who said she was?

MAE:
She did.

GOOPER:
The doctor didn't. Doc Baugh didn't.

MARGARET:
I haven't gone to Doc Baugh.

GOOPER:
Then who'd you go to, Maggie?

MARGARET:
One of the best gynecologists in the South.

GOOPER:
Uh-huh, uh-huh!—I see. . . .

> [*He takes out pencil and notebook.*]

—May we have his name, please?

MARGARET:
No, you may not, Mister Prosecuting Attorney!

MAE:
He doesn't have any name, he doesn't exist!

MARGARET:
Oh, he exists all right, and so does my child, Brick's baby!

MAE:
You can't conceive a child by a man that won't sleep with you unless you think you're—

> [*Brick has turned on the phonograph. A scat song cuts Mae's speech.*]

GOOPER:
Turn that off!

MAE:
We know it's a lie because we hear you in here; he won't sleep with you, we hear you! So don't imagine you're going to put a trick over on us, to fool a dying man with a—

> [*A long drawn cry of agony and rage fills the house. Margaret turns phonograph down to a whisper.*
> [*The cry is repeated.*]

MAE [*awed*]:
Did you hear that, Gooper, did you hear that?

GOOPER:
Sounds like the pain has struck.

MAE:
Go see, Gooper!

GOOPER:
Come along and leave these love birds together in their nest!

[*He goes out first. Mae follows but turns at the door, contorting her face and hissing at Margaret.*]

MAE:
Liar!

[*She slams the door.*
[*Margaret exhales with relief and moves a little un- steadily to catch hold of Brick's arm.*]

MARGARET:
Thank you for—keeping still . . .

BRICK:
OK, Maggie.

MARGARET:
It was gallant of you to save my face!

BRICK:
—It hasn't happened yet.

MARGARET:
What?

BRICK:
The click. . . .

MARGARET:
—the click in your head that makes you peaceful, honey?

BRICK:
Uh-huh. It hasn't happened. . . . I've got to make it happen before I can sleep. . . .

MARGARET:
—I—know what you—mean. . . .

BRICK:
Give me that pillow in the big chair, Maggie.

MARGARET:
I'll put it on the bed for you.

BRICK:
No, put it on the sofa, where I sleep.

MARGARET:
Not tonight, Brick.

BRICK:
I want it on the sofa. That's where I sleep.

> [*He has hobbled to the liquor cabinet. He now pours
> down three shots in quick succession and stands wait-
> ing, silent. All at once he turns with a smile and says:*]

There!

MARGARET:
What?

BRICK:
The *click.* . . .

> [*His gratitude seems almost infinite as he hobbles out
> on the gallery with a drink. We hear his crutch as he
> swings out of sight. Then, at some distance, he begins
> singing to himself a peaceful song.*
> [*Margaret holds the big pillow forlornly as if it were
> her only companion, for a few moments, then throws
> it on the bed. She rushes to the liquor cabinet, gathers
> all the bottles in her arms, turns about undecidedly,
> then runs out of the room with them, leaving the
> door ajar on the dim yellow hall. Brick is heard hob-
> bling back along the gallery, singing his peaceful
> song. He comes back in, sees the pillow on the bed,
> laughs lightly, sadly, picks it up. He has it under his
> arm as Margaret returns to the room. Margaret softly
> shuts the door and leans against it, smiling softly at
> Brick.*]

MARGARET:
Brick, I used to think that you were stronger than me
and I didn't want to be overpowered by you. But now,
since you've taken to liquor—you know what?—I guess
it's bad, but now I'm stronger than you and I can love
you more truly!
Don't move that pillow. I'll move it right back if you do!

—Brick?

[*She turns out all the lamps but a single rose-silk-shaded one by the bed.*]

I really have been to a doctor and I know what to do and—Brick?—this is my time by the calendar to conceive!

BRICK:

Yes, I understand, Maggie. But how are you going to conceive a child by a man in love with his liquor?

MARGARET:

By locking his liquor up and making him satisfy my desire before I unlock it!

BRICK:

Is that what you've done, Maggie?

MARGARET:

Look and see. That cabinet's mighty empty compared to before!

BRICK:

Well, I'll be a son of a—

[*He reaches for his crutch but she beats him to it and rushes out on the gallery, hurls the crutch over the rail and comes back in, panting.*

[*There are running footsteps. Big Mama bursts into the room, her face all awry, gasping, stammering.*]

BIG MAMA:

Oh, my God, oh, my God, oh, my God, where is it?

MARGARET:

Is this what you want, Big Mama?

[*Margaret hands her the package left by the doctor.*]

BIG MAMA:

I can't bear it, oh, God! Oh, Brick! Brick, baby!

[*She rushes at him. He averts his face from her sobbing kisses. Margaret watches with a tight smile.*]

My son, Big Daddy's boy! Little Father!

[*The groaning cry is heard again. She runs out, sobbing.*]

MARGARET:
And so tonight we're going to make the lie true, and
when that's done, I'll bring the liquor back here and
we'll get drunk together, here, tonight, in this place that
death has come into. . . .
—What do you say?

BRICK:
I don't say anything. I guess there's nothing to say.

MARGARET:
Oh, you weak people, you weak, beautiful people!—who
give up.—What you want is someone to—

[*She turns out the rose-silk lamp.*]

—take hold of you.—Gently, gently, with love! And—

[*The curtain begins to fall slowly.*]

I *do* love you, Brick, I *do!*

BRICK [*smiling with charming sadness*]:
Wouldn't it be funny if that was true?

THE CURTAIN COMES DOWN

THE END

NOTE OF EXPLANATION

Someday when time permits I would like to write a piece about the influence, its dangers and its values, of a powerful and highly imaginative director upon the development of a play, before and during production. It does have dangers, but it has them only if the playwright is excessively malleable or submissive, or the director is excessively insistent on ideas or interpretations of his own. Elia Kazan and I have enjoyed the advantages and avoided the dangers of this highly explosive relationship because of the deepest mutual respect for each other's creative function: we have worked together three times with a phenomenal absence of friction between us and each occasion has increased the trust.

If you don't want a director's influence on your play, there are two ways to avoid it, and neither is good. One way is to arrive at an absolutely final draft of your play before you let your director see it, then hand it to him saying, Here it is, take it or leave it! The other way is to select a director who is content to put your play on the stage precisely as you conceived it with no ideas of his own. I said neither is a good way, and I meant it. No living playwright, that I can think of, hasn't something valuable to learn about his own work from a director so keenly perceptive as Elia Kazan. It so happened that in the case of *Streetcar*, Kazan was given a script that was completely finished. In the case of *Cat*, he was shown the first typed version of the play, and he was excited by it, but he had definite reservations about it which were concentrated in the third act. The gist of his reservations can be listed as three points: one, he felt that

Big Daddy was too vivid and important a character to disappear from the play except as an offstage cry after the second act curtain; two, he felt that the character of Brick should undergo some apparent mutation as a result of the virtual vivisection that he undergoes in his interview with his father in Act Two. Three, he felt that the character of Margaret, while he understood that I sympathized with her and liked her myself, should be, if possible, more clearly sympathetic to an audience.

It was only the third of these suggestions that I embraced wholeheartedly from the outset, because it so happened that Maggie the Cat had become steadily more charming to me as I worked on her characterization. I didn't want Big Daddy to reappear in Act Three and I felt that the moral paralysis of Brick was a root thing in his tragedy, and to show a dramatic progression would obscure the meaning of that tragedy in him and because I don't believe that a conversation, however revelatory, ever effects so immediate a change in the heart or even conduct of a person in Brick's state of spiritual disrepair.

However, I wanted Kazan to direct the play, and though these suggestions were not made in the form of an ultimatum, I was fearful that I would lose his interest if I didn't reexamine the script from his point of view. I did. And you will find included in this published script the new third act that resulted from his creative influence on the play. The reception of the playing-script has more than justified, in my opinion, the adjustments made to that influence. A failure reaches fewer people, and touches fewer, than does a play that succeeds.

It may be that *Cat* number one would have done just as well, or nearly, as *Cat* number two; it's an interesting question. At any rate, with the publication of both third acts in this volume, the reader can, if he wishes, make up his own mind about it.

—Tennessee Williams

ACT THREE

AS PLAYED IN NEW YORK PRODUCTION

Big Daddy is seen leaving as at the end of Act II.

BIG DADDY [*shouts, as he goes out DR on gallery*]:
ALL—LYIN'—DYIN'—LIARS! LIARS! LIARS!

[*After Big Daddy has gone, Margaret enters from DR on gallery, into room through DS door. She X to Brick at LC.*]

MARGARET:
Brick, what in the name of God was goin' on in this room?

[*Dixie and Trixie rush through the room from the hall, L to gallery R, brandishing cap pistols, which they fire repeatedly, as they shout: "Bang! Bang! Bang!"*]

[*Mae appears from DR gallery entrance, and turns the children back UL, along gallery. At the same moment, Gooper, Reverend Tooker and Dr. Baugh enter from L in the hall.*]

MAE:
Dixie! You quit that! Gooper, will y'please git these kiddies t'baid? Right now?

[*Gooper and Reverend Tooker X along upper gallery. Dr. Baugh holds, UC, near hall door. Reverend Tooker X to Mae near section of gallery just outside doors, R.*]

GOOPER [*urging the children along*]:
Mae—you seen Big Mama?

MAE:
Not yet.

[*Dixie and Trixie vanish through hall, L.*]

REVEREND TOOKER [*to Mae*]:
Those kiddies are so full of vitality. I think I'll have to be startin' back to town.

[*Margaret turns to watch and listen.*]

MAE:
Not yet, Preacher. You know we regard you as a member of this fam'ly, one of our closest an' dearest, so you just got t'be with us when Doc Baugh gives Big Mama th' actual truth about th' report from th' clinic.

[*Calls through door:*]
Has Big Daddy gone to bed, Brick?

[*Gooper has gone out DR at the beginning of the exchange between Mae and Reverend Tooker.*]

MARGARET [*replying to Mae*]:
Yes, he's gone to bed.

[*To Brick:*]
Why'd Big Daddy shout "liars"?

GOOPER [*off DR*]:
Mae!

[*Mae exits DR. Reverend Tooker drifts along upper gallery.*]

BRICK:
I didn't lie to Big Daddy. I've lied to nobody, nobody but myself, just lied to myself. The time has come to put me in Rainbow Hill, put me in Rainbow Hill, Maggie, I ought to go there.

MARGARET:
Over my dead body!

[*Brick starts R. She holds him.*]
Where do you think you're goin'?

[*Mae enters from DR on gallery, X to Reverend Tooker, who comes to meet her.*]

BRICK [*X below to C*]:
Out for some air, I want air—

GOOPER [*entering from DR to Mae, on gallery*]:
Now, where is that old lady?

MAE:
Cantcha find her, Gooper?

 [*Reverend Tooker goes out DR.*]

GOOPER [*X to Doc above hall door*]:
She's avoidin' this talk.

MAE:
I think she senses somethin'.

GOOPER [*calls off L*]:
Sookey! Go find Big Mama an' tell her Doc Baugh an'
the Preacher've got to go soon.

MAE:
Don't let Big Daddy hear yuh!

 [*Brings Dr. Baugh to R on gallery.*]

REVEREND TOOKER [*off DR, calls*]:
Big Mama.

SOOKEY and DAISY [*running from L to R on lawn,
calling*]:
Miss Ida! Miss Ida!

 [*They go out UR.*]

GOOPER [*calling off upper gallery*]:
Lacey, you look downstairs for Big Mama!

MARGARET:
Brick, they're going to tell Big Mama the truth now, an'
she needs you!

 [*Reverend Tooker appears in lawn area, UR, X C.*]

DOCTOR BAUGH [*to Mae, on R gallery*]:
This is going to be painful.

MAE:
Painful things can't always be avoided.

DOCTOR BAUGH:
That's what I've noticed about 'em, Sister Woman.

REVEREND TOOKER [*on lawn, points off R*]:
I see Big Mama!

 [*Hurries off L and reappears shortly in hall.*]

GOOPER [*hurrying into hall*]:
She's gone round the gall'ry to' Big Daddy's room.
Hey, Mama!

 [*Off:*]

Hey, Big Mama! Come here!

MAE [*calls*]:
Hush, Gooper! Don't holler, go to her!

 [*Gooper and Reverend Tooker now appear together
 in hall. Big Mama runs in from DR, carrying a glass
 of milk. She X past Dr. Baugh to Mae, on R gallery.
 Dr. Baugh turns away.*]

BIG MAMA:
Here I am! What d'you all want with me?

GOOPER [*steps toward Big Mama*]:
Big Mama, I told you we got to have this talk.

BIG MAMA:
What talk you talkin' about? I saw the light go on in
Big Daddy's bedroom an' took him his glass of milk, an'
he just shut the shutters right in my face.

 [*Steps into room through R door.*]

When old couples have been together as long as me an'
Big Daddy, they, they get irritable with each other just
from too much—devotion! Isn't that so?

 [*X below wicker seat to RC area.*]

MARGARET [*X to Big Mama, embracing her*]:
Yes, of course it's so.

 [*Brick starts out UC through hall, but sees Gooper
 and Reverend Tooker entering, so he hobbles
 through C out DS door and onto gallery.*]

BIG MAMA:
I think Big Daddy was just worn out. He loves his
fam'ly. He loves to have 'em around him, but it's a strain
on his nerves. He wasn't himself tonight, Brick—
> [*XC toward Brick. Brick passes her on his way
> out, DS.*]

Big Daddy wasn't himself, I could tell he was all
worked up.

REVEREND TOOKER [*USC*]:
I think he's remarkable.

BIG MAMA:
Yaiss! Just remarkable.
> [*Faces US, turns, X to bar, puts down glass of milk.*]

Did you notice all the food he ate at that table?
> [*XR a bit.*]

Why he ate like a hawss!

GOOPER [*USC*]:
I hope he don't regret it.

BIG MAMA [*turns US toward Gooper*]:
What! Why that man ate a huge piece of cawn bread
with molasses on it! Helped himself twice to hoppin'
john!

MARGARET [*X to Big Mama*]:
Big Daddy loves hoppin' john. We had a real country
dinner.

BIG MAMA:
Yais, he simply adores it! An' candied yams. Son—
> [*X to DS door, looking out at Brick. Margaret X
> above Big Mama to her L.*]

That man put away enough food at that table to stuff a
field-hand.

GOOPER:
I hope he don't have to pay for it later on.

BIG MAMA [*turns US*]:
What's that, Gooper?

MAE:
Gooper says he hopes Big Daddy doesn't suffer tonight.

BIG MAMA [*turns to Margaret, DC*]:
Oh, shoot, Gooper says, Gooper says! Why should Big
Daddy suffer for satisfyin' a nawmal appetite? There's
nothin' wrong with that man but nerves; he's sound as a
dollar! An' now he knows he is, an' that's why he ate such
a supper. He had a big load off his mind, knowin' he wasn't
doomed to—what—he thought he was—doomed t'—

> [*She wavers.*
> [*Margaret puts her arms around Big Mama.*]

GOOPER [*urging Mae forward*]:
MAE!

> [*Mae runs forward below wicker seat. She stands
> below Big Mama, Margaret above Big Mama. They
> help her to the wicker seat. Big Mama sits. Margaret
> sits above her. Mae stands behind her.*]

MARGARET:
Bless his ole sweet soul.

BIG MAMA:
Yes—bless his heart.

BRICK [*DS on gallery, looking out front*]:
Hello, moon, I envy you, you cool son of a bitch.

BIG MAMA:
I want Brick!

MARGARET:
He just stepped out for some fresh air.

BIG MAMA:
Honey! I want Brick!

MAE:
Bring li'l Brother in here so we kin talk.

> [*Margaret rises, X through DS door to Brick on
> gallery.*]

BRICK [*to the moon*]:
I envy you—you cool son of a bitch.

MARGARET:
Brick, what're you doin' out here on the gall'ry, Baby?

BRICK:
Admirin' an' complimentin' th' man in the moon.

[*Mae X to Dr. Baugh on R gallery. Reverend Tooker and Gooper move R UC, looking at Big Mama.*]

MARGARET [*to Brick*]:
Come in, Baby. They're gettin' ready to tell Big Mama the truth.

BRICK:
I can't witness that thing in there.

MAE:
Doc Baugh, d'you think those vitamin B_{12} injections are all they're cracked up t'be?

[*Enters room to upper side, behind wicker seat.*]

DOCTOR BAUGH [*X to below wicker seat*]:
Well, I guess they're as good t'be stuck with as anything else.

[*Looks at watch; X through to LC.*]

MARGARET [*to Brick*]:
Big Mama needs you!

BRICK:
I can't witness that thing in there!

BIG MAMA:
What's wrong here? You all have such long faces, you sit here waitin' for somethin' like a bomb—to go off.

GOOPER:
We're waitin' for Brick an' Maggie to come in for this talk.

MARGARET [*X above Brick, to his R*]:
Brother Man an' Mae have got a trick up their sleeves, an' if you don't go in there t'help Big Mama, y'know what I'm goin' to do—?

BIG MAMA:
Talk. Whispers! Whispers!

[*Looks out DR.*]

Brick! . . .

MARGARET [*answering Big Mama's call*]:
Comin', Big Mama!

[*To Brick:*]

I'm goin' to take every damn bottle on this place an' pitch it off th' levee into th' river!

BIG MAMA:
Never had this sort of atmosphere here before.

MAE [*sits above Big Mama on wicker seat*]:
Before what, Big Mama?

BIG MAMA:
This occasion. What's Brick an' Maggie doin' out there now?

GOOPER [*X DC, looks out*]:
They seem to be havin' some little altercation.

[*Brick X toward DS step. Maggie moves R above him to portal DR. Reverend Tooker joins Dr. Baugh, LC.*]

BIG MAMA [*taking a pill from pill box on chain at her wrist*]:
Give me a little somethin' to wash this tablet down with. Smell of burnt fireworks always makes me sick.

[*Mae X to bar to pour glass of water. Dr. Baugh joins her. Gooper X to Reverend Tooker, LC.*]

BRICK [*to Maggie*]:
You're a live cat, aren't you?

MARGARET:
You're damn right I am!

BIG MAMA:
Gooper, will y'please open that hall door—an' let some air circulate in this stiflin' room?

[*Gooper starts US, but is restrained by Mae who X*]

through C with glass of water. Gooper turns to men DLC.]

MAE [*X to Big Mama with water, sits above her*]:
Big Mama, I think we ought to keep that door closed till after we talk.

BIG MAMA:
I swan!

[*Drinks water. Washes down pill.*]

MAE:
I just don't think we ought to take any chance of Big Daddy hearin' a word of this discussion.

BIG MAMA [*hands glass to Mae*]:
What discussion of what? Maggie! Brick! Nothin' is goin' to be said in th' house of Big Daddy Pollitt that he can't hear if he wants to!

[*Mae rises, X to bar, puts down glass, joins Gooper and the two men, LC.*]

BRICK:
How long are you goin' to stand behind me, Maggie?

MARGARET:
Forever, if necessary.

[*Brick X US to R gallery door.*]

BIG MAMA:
Brick!

[*Mae rises, looks out DS, sits.*]

GOOPER:
That boy's gone t'pieces—he's just gone t'pieces.

DOCTOR BAUGH:
Y'know, in my day they used to have somethin' they called the Keeley cure for drinkers.

BIG MAMA:
Shoot!

DOCTOR BAUGH:
But nowadays, I understand they take some kind of tablets that kill their taste for the stuff.

GOOPER [*turns to Dr. Baugh*]:
Call 'em anti-bust tablets.

BIG MAMA:
Brick don't need to take nothin'. That boy is just broken up over Skipper's death. You know how poor Skipper died. They gave him a big, big dose of that sodium amytal stuff at his home an' then they called the ambulance an' give him another big, big dose of it at th' hospital an' that an' all the alcohol in his system fo' months an' months just proved too much for his heart an' his heart quit beatin'. I'm scared of needles! I'm more scared of a needle than th' knife—

[*Brick has entered the room to behind the wicker seat. He rests his hand on Big Mama's head. Gooper has moved a bit URC, facing Big Mama.*]

Oh! Here's Brick! My precious baby!

[*Dr. Baugh X to bar, puts down drink. Brick X below Big Mama through C to bar.*]

BRICK:
Take it, Gooper!

MAE [*rising*]:
What?

BRICK:
Gooper knows what. Take it, Gooper!

[*Mae turns to Gooper URC. Dr. Baugh X to Reverend Tooker. Margaret, who has followed Brick US on R gallery before he entered the room, now enters room, to behind wicker seat.*]

BIG MAMA [*to Brick*]:
You just break my heart.

BRICK [*at bar*]:
Sorry—anyone else?

MARGARET:
Brick, sit with Big Mama an' hold her hand while we talk.

BRICK:
You do that, Maggie. I'm a restless cripple. I got to stay on my crutch.

> [*Mae sits above Big Mama. Gooper moves in front, below, and sits on couch, facing Big Mama. Reverend Tooker closes in to RC. Dr. Baugh X DC, faces upstage, smoking cigar. Margaret turns away to R doors.*]

BIG MAMA:
Why're you all *surroundin'* me?—like this? Why're you all starin' at me like this an' makin' signs at each other?

> [*Brick hobbles out hall door and X along R gallery.*]

I don't need nobody to hold my hand. Are you all crazy? Since when did Big Daddy or me need anybody—?

> [*Reverend Tooker moves behind wicker seat.*]

MAE:
Calm yourself, Big Mama.

BIG MAMA:
Calm you'self *you'self*, Sister Woman! How could I calm myself with everyone starin' at me as if big drops of blood had broken out on m'face? What's this all about, Annh! What?

GOOPER:
Doc Baugh—

> [*Mae rises.*]

Sit down, Mae—

> [*Mae sits.*]

—Big Mama wants to know the complete truth about th' report we got today from the Ochsner Clinic!

> [*Dr. Baugh buttons his coat, faces group at RC.*]

BIG MAMA:
Is there somethin'—somethin' that I don't know?

DOCTOR BAUGH:
Yes—well . . .

BIG MAMA [*rises*]:
I—want to—*knowwwww!*
　　[*X to Dr. Baugh.*]
Somebody must be lyin'! *I want to know!*
　　[*Mae, Gooper, Reverend Tooker surround Big Mama.*]

MAE:
Sit down, Big Mama, sit down on this sofa!
　　[*Brick has passed Margaret Xing DR on gallery.*]

MARGARET:
Brick! Brick!

BIG MAMA:
What is it, what is it?
　　[*Big Mama drives Dr. Baugh a bit DLC. Others fol-
　　low, surrounding Big Mama.*]

DOCTOR BAUGH:
I never have seen a more thorough examination than
Big Daddy Pollit was given in all my experience at the
Ochsner Clinic.

GOOPER:
It's one of th' best in th' country.

MAE:
It's *THE* best in th' country—bar none!

DOCTOR BAUGH:
Of course they were ninety-nine and nine-tenths per cent
certain before they even started.

BIG MAMA:
Sure of what, sure of what, sure of what—*what!?*

MAE:
Now, Mommy, be a brave girl!

BRICK [*on DR gallery, covers his ears, sings*]:
By the light, by the light, of the silvery moon!

GOOPER [breaks DR. Calls out to Brick]:
Shut up, Brick!
　　[Returns to group LC.]

BRICK:
Sorry . . .
　　[Continues singing.]

DOCTOR BAUGH:
But now, you see, Big Mama, they cut a piece off this growth, a specimen of the tissue, an'—

BIG MAMA:
Growth? You told Big Daddy—

DOCTOR BAUGH:
Now, wait—

BIG MAMA:
You told me an' Big Daddy there wasn't a thing wrong with him but—

MAE:
Big Mama, they always—

GOOPER:
Let Doc Baugh talk, will yuh?

BIG MAMA:
—little spastic condition of—

REVEREND TOOKER [throughout all this]:
Shh! Shh! Shh!
　　[Big Mama breaks UC, they all follow.]

DOCTOR BAUGH:
Yes, that's what we told Big Daddy. But we had this bit of tissue run through the laboratory an' I'm sorry t'say the test was positive on it. It's malignant.
　　[Pause.]

BIG MAMA:
Cancer! Cancer!

MAE:
Now now, Mommy—

GOOPER [*at the same time*]:
You had to know, Big Mama.

BIG MAMA:
Why didn't they cut it out of him? Hanh? Hannh?

DOCTOR BAUGH:
Involved too much, Big Mama, too many organs affected.

MAE:
Big Mama, the liver's affected, an' so's the kidneys, both. It's gone way past what they call a—

GOOPER:
—a surgical risk.
    [*Big Mama gasps.*]

REVEREND TOOKER:
Tch, tch, tch.

DOCTOR BAUGH:
Yes, it's gone past the knife.

MAE:
That's why he's turned yellow!
    [*Brick stops singing, turns away UR on gallery.*]

BIG MAMA [*pushes Mae DS*]:
Git away from me, git away from me, Mae!
    [*X DSR.*]
I want Brick! Where's Brick! *Where's my only son?*

MAE [*a step after Big Mama*]:
Mama! Did she say "only" son?

GOOPER [*following Big Mama*]:
What does that make me?

MAE [*above Gooper*]:
A sober responsible man with five precious children—
six!

BIG MAMA:
I want Brick! Brick! Brick!

MARGARET [*a step to Big Mama above couch*]:
Mama, let *me* tell you.

BIG MAMA [*pushing her aside*]:
No, no, leave me alone, you're not my blood!
    [*She rushes onto the DS gallery.*]

GOOPER [*X to Big Mama on gallery*]:
Mama! I'm your son! Listen to me!

MAE:
Gooper's your son, Mama, he's your first-born!

BIG MAMA:
Gooper never liked Daddy!

MAE:
That's not true!

REVEREND TOOKER [*UC*]:
I think I'd better slip away at this point. Goodnight,
goodnight everybody, and God bless you all—on this
place.

    [*Goes out through hall.*]

DOCTOR BAUGH [*X DR to above DS door*]:
Well, Big Mama—

BIG MAMA [*leaning against Gooper, on lower gallery*]:
It's all a mistake, I know it's just a bad dream.

DOCTOR BAUGH:
We're gonna keep Big Daddy as comfortable as we can.

BIG MAMA:
Yes, it's just a bad dream, that's all it is, it's just an
awful dream.

GOOPER:
In my opinion Big Daddy is havin' some pain but won't
admit that he has it.

BIG MAMA:
Just a dream, a bad dream.

DOCTOR BAUGH:
That's what lots of 'em do, they think if they don't admit

they're havin' the pain they can sort of escape th' fact
of it.

> [*Brick X US on R gallery. Margaret watches him
> from R door.*]

GOOPER:
Yes, they get sly about it, get real sly about it.

MAE [*X to R of Dr. Baugh*]:
Gooper an' I think—

GOOPER:
Shut up, Mae!—Big Mama, I really do think Big Daddy
should be started on morphine.

BIG MAMA [*pulling away from Gooper*]:
Nobody's goin' to give Big Daddy morphine!

DOCTOR BAUGH:
Now, Big Mama, when that pain strikes it's goin' to
strike mighty hard an' Big Daddy's goin' t'need the needle to bear it.

BIG MAMA [*X to Dr. Baugh*]:
I tell you, nobody's goin' to give him morphine!

MAE:
Big Mama, you don't want to see Big Daddy suffer,
y'know y'—

DOCTOR BAUGH [*X to bar*]:
Well, I'm leavin' this stuff here—

> [*Puts packet of morphine, etc., on bar.*]

—so if there's a sudden attack you won't have to send
out for it.

> [*Big Mama hurries to L side bar.*]

MAE [*X C, below Dr. Baugh*]:
I know how to give a hypo.

BIG MAMA:
Nobody's goin' to give Big Daddy morphine!

GOOPER [*X C*]:
Mae took a course in nursin' durin' th' war.

MARGARET:
Somehow I don't think Big Daddy would want Mae t'give him a hypo.

MAE [*to Margaret*]:
You think he'd want *you* to do it?

DOCTOR BAUGH:
Well—

GOOPER:
Well, Doc Baugh is goin'—

DOCTOR BAUGH:
Yes, I got to be goin'. Well, keep your chin up, Big Mama.

    [*X to hall.*]

GOOPER [*as he and Mae follow Dr. Baugh into the hall*]:
She's goin' to keep her ole chin up, aren't you, Big Mama?

    [*They go out L.*]
Well, Doc, we sure do appreciate all you've done. I'm telling you, we're obligated—

BIG MAMA:
Margaret!

    [*XRC.*]

MARGARET [*meeting Big Mama in front of wicker seat*]:
I'm right here, Big Mama.

BIG MAMA:
Margaret, you've got to cooperate with me an' Big Daddy to straighten Brick out now—

GOOPER [*off L, returning with Mae*]:
I guess that Doctor has got a lot on his mind, but it wouldn't hurt him to act a little more human—

BIG MAMA:
—because it'll break Big Daddy's heart if Brick don't pull himself together an' take hold of things here.

    [*Brick X DSR on gallery.*]

MAE [*UC, overhearing*]:
Take hold of what things, Big Mama?

BIG MAMA [*sits in wicker chair, Margaret standing behind chair*]:
The place.

GOOPER [*UC*]:
Big Mama, you've had a shock.

MAE [*X with Gooper to Big Mama*]:
Yais, we've all had a shock, but—

GOOPER:
Let's be realistic—

MAE:
Big Daddy would not, would *never,* be foolish enough to—

GOOPER:
—put this place in irresponsible hands!

BIG MAMA:
Big Daddy ain't goin' t'put th' place in anybody's hands, Big Daddy is *not* goin' t'die! I want you to git that into your haids, all of you!

> [*Mae sits above Big Mama, Margaret turns R to door, Gooper X LC a bit.*]

MAE:
Mommy, Mommy, Big Mama, we're just as hopeful an' optimistic as you are about Big Daddy's prospects, we have faith in prayer—but nevertheless there are certain matters that have to be discussed an' dealt with, because otherwise—

GOOPER:
Mae, will y'please get my briefcase out of our room?

MAE:
Yes, honey.

> [*Rises, goes out through hall L.*]

MARGARET [*X to Brick on DS gallery*]:
Hear them in there?

[*X back to R gallery door.*]

GOOPER [*stands above Big Mama. Leaning over her*]:
Big Mama, what you said just now was not at all true,
an' you know it. I've always loved Big Daddy in my own
quiet way. I never made a show of it. I know that Big
Daddy has always been fond of me in a quiet way, too.

[*Margaret drifts UR on gallery. Mae returns, X to
Gooper's L with briefcase.*]

MAE:
Here's your briefcase, Gooper, honey.

[*Hands it to him.*]

GOOPER [*hands briefcase back to Mae*]:
Thank you. Of cou'se, my relationship with Big Daddy
is different from Brick's.

MAE:
You're eight years older'n Brick an' always had t'carry
a bigger load of th' responsibilities than Brick ever had
t'carry; he never carried a thing in his life but a football
or a highball.

GOOPER:
Mae, will y'let me talk, please?

MAE:
Yes, honey.

GOOPER:
Now, a twenty-eight-thousand-acre plantation's a mighty
big thing t'run.

MAE:
Almost single-handed!

BIG MAMA:
You never had t'run this place, Brother Man, what're
you talkin' about, as if Big Daddy was dead an' in his
grave, you had to run it? Why, you just had t'help him
out with a few business details an' had your law practice
at the same time in Memphis.

MAE:
Oh, Mommy, Mommy, Mommy! Let's be fair! Why, Gooper has given himself body an' soul t'keepin' this place up fo' the past five years since Big Daddy's health started failin'. Gooper won't say it, Gooper never thought of it as a duty, he just did it. An' what did Brick do? Brick kep' livin' in his past glory at college!

[*Gooper places a restraining hand on Mae's leg; Margaret drifts DS in gallery.*]

GOOPER:
Still a football player at twenty-seven!

MARGARET [*bursts into UR door*]:
Who are you talkin' about now? Brick? A football player? He isn't a football player an' you know it! Brick is a sports announcer on TV an' one of the best-known ones in the country!

MAE [*breaks UC*]:
I'm talkin' about what he was!

MARGARET [*X to above lower gallery door*]:
Well, I wish you would just stop talkin' about my husband!

GOOPER [*X to above Margaret*]:
Listen, Margaret, I've got a right to discuss my own brother with other members of my own fam'ly, which don't include *you!*

[*Pokes finger at her; she slaps his finger away.*]
Now, why don't you go on out there an' drink with Brick?

MARGARET:
I've never seen such malice toward a brother.

GOOPER:
How about his for me? Why he can't stand to be in the same room with me!

BRICK [*on lower gallery*]:
That's the truth!

MARGARET:

This is a deliberate campaign of vilification for the most disgusting and sordid reason on earth, and I know what it is! *It's avarice, avarice, greed, greed!*

BIG MAMA:

Oh, I'll scream, I will scream in a moment unless this stops! Margaret, child, come here, sit next to Big Mama.

MARGARET [*X to Big Mama, sits above her*]:
Precious Mommy.

[*Gooper X to bar.*]

MAE:

How beautiful, how touchin' this display of devotion! Do you know why she's childless? She's childless because that big, beautiful athlete husband of hers won't go to bed with her, that's why!

[*X to L of bed, looks at Gooper.*]

GOOPER:

You jest won't let me do this the nice way, will yuh? Aw right—

[*X to above wicker seat.*]

I don't give a goddam if Big Daddy likes me or don't like me or did or never did or will or will never! I'm just appealin' to a sense of common decency an' fair play! I'm tellin' you th' truth—

[*X DS through lower door to Brick on DR gallery.*]

I've resented Big Daddy's partiality to Brick ever since th' goddam day you were born, son, an' th' way I've been treated, like I was just barely good enough to spit on, an' sometimes not even good enough for that.

[*X back through room to above wicker seat.*]

Big Daddy is dyin' of cancer an' it's spread all through him an' it's attacked all his vital organs includin' the kidneys an' right now he is sinkin' into uremia, an' you all know what uremia is, it's poisonin' of the whole system due to th' failure of th' body to eliminate its poisons.

MARGARET:
Poisons, poisons, venomous thoughts and words! In hearts and minds! That's poisons!

GOOPER:
I'm askin' for a square deal an' by God I expect to get one. But if I don't get one, if there's any peculiar shenanigans goin' on around here behind my back, well I'm not a corporation lawyer for nothin'!

[*X DS toward lower gallery door, on apex.*]

I know how to protect my own interests.

[*Rumble of distant thunder.*]

BRICK [*entering the room through DS door*]:
Storm comin' up.

GOOPER:
Oh, a late arrival!

MAE [*X through C to below bar, LCO*]:
Behold, the conquerin' hero comes!

GOOPER [*X through C to bar, following Brick, imitating his limp*]:
The fabulous Brick Pollitt! Remember him? Who could forget him?

MAE:
He looks like he's been injured in a game!

GOOPER:
Yep, I'm afraid you'll have to warm th' bench at the Sugar Bowl this year, Brick! Or was it the Rose Bowl that he made his famous run in.

[*Another rumble of thunder, sound of wind rising.*]

MAE [*X to L of Brick, who has reached the bar*]:
The punch bowl, honey, it was the punch bowl, the cut-glass punch bowl!

GOOPER:
That's right! I'm always gettin' the boy's *bowls* mixed up!

[*Pats Brick on the butt.*]

MARGARET [*rushes at Gooper, striking him*]:
Stop that! You stop that!

> [*Thunder.*
> [*Mae X toward Margaret from L of Gooper, flails at Margaret; Gooper keeps the women apart. Lacey runs through the US lawn area in a raincoat.*]

DAISY and SOOKEY [*off UL*]:
Storm! Storm comin'! Storm! Storm!

LACEY [*running out UR*]:
Brightie, close them shutters!

GOOPER [*X onto R gallery, calls after Lacey*]:
Lacey, put the top up on my Cadillac, will yuh?

LACEY [*off R*]:
Yes, suh, Mistah Pollitt!

GOOPER [*X to above Big Mama*]:
Big Mama, you know it's goin' to be necessary for me t'go back to Memphis in th' mornin' t'represent the Parker estate in a lawsuit.

> [*Mae sits on L side bed, arranges papers she removes from briefcase.*]

BIG MAMA:
Is it, Gooper?

MAE:
Yaiss.

GOOPER:
That's why I'm forced to—to bring up a problem that—

MAE:
Somethin' that's too important t' be put off!

GOOPER:
If Brick was sober, he ought to be in on this. I think he ought to be present when I present this plan.

MARGARET [*UC*]:
Brick is present, we're present!

GOOPER:
Well, good. I will now give you this outline my partner, Tom Bullit, an' me have drawn up—a sort of dummy—trusteeship!

MARGARET:
Oh, that's it! You'll be in charge an' dole out remittances, will you?

GOOPER:
This we did as soon as we got the report on Big Daddy from th' Ochsner Laboratories. We did this thing, I mean we drew up this dummy outline with the advice and assistance of the Chairman of the Boa'd of Directors of th' Southern Plantuhs Bank and Trust Company in Memphis, C. C. Bellowes, a man who handles estates for all th' prominent fam'lies in West Tennessee and th' Delta!

BIG MAMA:
Gooper?

GOOPER [X behind seat to below Big Mama]:
Now this is not—not final, or anything like it, this is just a preliminary outline. But it does provide a—basis—a design—a—possible, feasible—plan!

[He waves papers Mae has thrust into his hand, US.]

MARGARET [X DL]:
Yes, I'll bet it's a plan!

[Thunder rolls. Interior lighting dims.]

MAE:
It's a plan to protect the biggest estate in the Delta from irresponsibility an'—

BIG MAMA:
Now you listen to me, all of you, you listen here! They's not goin' to be no more catty talk in my house! And Gooper, you put that away before I grab it out of your hand and tear it right up! I don't know what the hell's in it, and I don't want to know what the hell's in it. I'm talkin' in Big Daddy's language now, I'm his wife, not

his *widow,* I'm still his *wife!* And I'm talkin' to you in
his language an'—

GOOPER:
Big Mama, what I have here is—

MAE:
Gooper explained that it's just a plan . . .

BIG MAMA:
I don't care what you got there, just put it back where
it come from an' don't let me see it again, not even the
outside of the envelope of it! Is that understood? Basis!
Plan! Preliminary! Design!—I say—what is it that Big
Daddy always says when he's disgusted?

   [*Storm clouds race across sky.*]

BRICK [*from bar*]:
Big Daddy says "crap" when he is disgusted.

BIG MAMA [*rising*]:
That's right—*CRAPPPP!* I say *CRAP* too, like Big
Daddy!

   [*Thunder rolls.*]

MAE:
Coarse language don't seem called for in this—

GOOPER:
Somethin' in me is *deeply outraged* by this.

BIG MAMA:
Nobody's goin' to do nothin'! till Big Daddy lets go of
it, and maybe just possibly not—not even then! No, not
even then!

   [*Thunder clap. Glass crash, off L.*
   [*Off UR, children commence crying. Many storm
   sounds, L and R: barnyard animals in terror, papers
   crackling, shutters rattling. Sookey and Daisy hurry
   from L to R in lawn area. Inexplicably, Daisy hits
   together two leather pillows. They cry, "Storm!
   Storm!" Sookey waves a piece of wrapping paper to
   cover lawn furniture. Mae exits to hall and upper
   gallery. Strange man runs across lawn, R to L.*

[*Thunder rolls repeatedly.*]

MAE:
Sookey, hurry up an' git that po'ch fu'niture covahed; want th' paint to come off?

　　[*Starts DR on gallery.*
　　[*Gooper runs through hall to R gallery.*]

GOOPER [*yells to Lacey, who appears from R*]:
Lacey, put mah car away!

LACEY:
Cain't, Mistah Pollitt, you got the keys!

　　[*Exit US.*]

GOOPER:
Naw, you got 'em, man.

　　[*Exit DR. Reappears UR, calls to Mae:*]
Where th' keys to th' car, honey?

　　[*Runs C.*]

MAE [*DR on gallery*]:
You got 'em in your pocket!

　　[*Exit DR.*
　　[*Gooper exits UR. Dog howls. Daisy and Sookey sing off UR to comfort children. Mae is heard placating the children.*
　　[*Storm fades away.*
　　[*During the storm, Margaret X and sits on couch, DR. Big Mama X DC.*]

BIG MAMA:
BRICK! Come here, Brick, I need you.

　　[*Thunder distantly.*
　　[*Children whimper, off L. Mae consoles them. Brick X to R of Big Mama.*]

BIG MAMA:
Tonight Brick looks like he used to look when he was a little boy just like he did when he played wild games in the orchard back of the house and used to come home when I hollered myself hoarse for him! all—sweaty—and pink-cheeked—an' sleepy with his curls shinin'—

[*Thunder distantly.*
[*Children whimper, off L. Mae consoles them. Dog howls, off.*]

Time goes by so fast. Nothin' can outrun it. Death commences too early—almost before you're half-acquainted with life—you meet with the other. Oh, you know we just got to love each other, an' stay together all of us just as close as we can, specially now that such a *black* thing has come and moved into this place without invitation.

[*Dog howls, off.*]

Oh, Brick, son of Big Daddy, Big Daddy does so love you. Y'know what would be his fondest dream come true? If before he passed on, if Big Daddy has to pass on . . .

[*Dog howls, off.*]

You give him a child of yours, a grandson as much like his son as his son is like Big Daddy. . . .

MARGARET:
I know that's Big Daddy's dream.

BIG MAMA:
That's his dream.

BIG DADDY [*off DR on gallery*]:
Looks like the wind was takin' liberties with this place.

[*Lacey appears UL, X to UC in lawn area; Brightie and Small appear UR on lawn. Big Daddy X onto the UR gallery.*]

LACEY:
Evenin', Mr. Pollitt.

BRIGHTIE and SMALL:
Evenin', Cap'n. Hello, Cap'n.

MARGARET [*X to R door*]:
Big Daddy's on the gall'ry.

BIG DADDY:
Stawm crossed th' river, Lacey?

LACEY:
Gone to Arkansas, Cap'n.

> [*Big Mama has turned toward the hall door at the sound of Big Daddy's voice on the gallery. Now she X's DSR and out the DS door onto the gallery.*]

BIG MAMA:
I can't stay here. He'll see somethin' in my eyes.

BIG DADDY [*on upper gallery, to the boys*]:
Stawm done any damage around here?

BRIGHTIE:
Took the po'ch off ole Aunt Crawley's house.

BIG DADDY:
Ole Aunt Crawley should of been settin' on it. It's time fo' th' wind to blow that ole girl away!

> [*Field-hands laugh, exit, UR. Big Daddy enters room, UC, hall door.*]

Can I come in?

> [*Puts his cigar in ash tray on bar.*
> [*Mae and Gooper hurry along the upper gallery and stand behind Big Daddy in hall door.*]

MARGARET:
Did the storm wake you up, Big Daddy?

BIG DADDY:
Which stawm are you talkin' about—th' one outside or th' hullaballoo in here?

> [*Gooper squeezes past Big Daddy.*]

GOOPER [*X toward bed, where legal papers are strewn*]:
'Scuse me, sir . . .

> [*Mae tries to squeeze past Big Daddy to join Gooper, but Big Daddy puts his arm firmly around her.*]

BIG DADDY:
I heard some mighty loud talk. Sounded like somethin' important was bein' discussed. What was the powwow about?

MAE [*flustered*]:
Why—nothin', Big Daddy . . .

BIG DADDY [*X DLC, taking Mae with him*]:
What is that pregnant-lookin' envelope you're puttin'
back in your briefcase, Gooper?

GOOPER [*at foot of bed, caught, as he stuffs papers into
envelope*]:
That? Nothin', suh—nothin' much of anythin' at all . . .

BIG DADDY:
Nothin'? It looks like a whole lot of nothing!
   [*Turns US to group:*]
You all know th' story about th' young married couple—

GOOPER:
Yes, sir!

BIG DADDY:
Hello, Brick—

BRICK:
Hello, Big Daddy.
   [*The group is arranged in a semi-circle above Big
   Daddy, Margaret at the extreme R, then Mae and
   Gooper, then Big Mama, with Brick at L.*]

BIG DADDY:
Young married couple took Junior out to th' zoo one
Sunday, inspected all of God's creatures in their cages,
with satisfaction.

GOOPER:
Satisfaction.

BIG DADDY [*X USC, face front*]:
This afternoon was a warm afternoon in spring an' that
ole elephant had somethin' else on his mind which was
bigger'n peanuts. You know this story, Brick?
   [*Gooper nods.*]

BRICK:
No, sir, I don't know it.

BIG DADDY:
Y'see, in th' cage adjoinin' they was a young female elephant in heat!

BIG MAMA [*at Big Daddy's shoulder*]:
Oh, Big Daddy!

BIG DADDY:
What's the matter, preacher's gone, ain't he? All right. That female elephant in the next cage was permeatin' the atmosphere about her with a powerful and excitin' odor of female fertility! Huh! Ain't that a nice way to put it, Brick?

BRICK:
Yes, sir, nothin' wrong with it.

BIG DADDY:
Brick says the's nothin' wrong with it!

BIG MAMA:
Oh, Big Daddy!

BIG DADDY [*X DSC*]:
So this ole bull elephant still had a couple of fornications left in him. He reared back his trunk an' got a whiff of that elephant lady next door!—began to paw at the dirt in his cage an' butt his head against the separatin' partition and, first thing y'know, there was a conspicuous change in his *profile*—very *conspicuous!* Ain't I tellin' this story in decent language, Brick?

BRICK:
Yes, sir, too ruttin' decent!

BIG DADDY:
So, the little boy pointed at it and said, "What's that?" His mam said, "Oh, that's—nothin'!"—His Papa said, "She's spoiled!"

> [*Field-hands sing off R, featuring Sookey: "I Just Can't Stay Here by Myself," through following scene.*
> [*Big Daddy X to Brick at L.*]

You didn't laugh at that story, Brick.

[*Big Mama X DRC crying. Margaret goes to her. Mae and Gooper hold URC.*]

BRICK:

No, sir, I didn't laugh at that story.

[*On the lower gallery, Big Mama sobs. Big Daddy looks toward her.*]

BIG DADDY:

What's wrong with that long, thin woman over there, loaded with diamonds? Hey, what's-your-name, what's the matter with you?

MARGARET [*X toward Big Daddy*]:

She had a slight dizzy spell, Big Daddy.

BIG DADDY [*ULC*]:

You better watch that, Big Mama. A stroke is a bad way to go.

MARGARET [*X to Big Daddy at C*]:

Oh, Brick, Big Daddy has on your birthday present to him, Brick, he has on your cashmere robe, the softest material I have ever felt.

BIG DADDY:

Yeah, this is my soft birthday, Maggie. . . .
Not my gold or my silver birthday, but my soft birthday, everything's got to be soft for Big Daddy on this soft birthday.

[*Maggie kneels before Big Daddy C. As Gooper and Mae speak, Big Mama X USRC in front of them, hushing them with a gesture.*]

GOOPER:

Maggie, I hate to make such a crude observation, but there is somethin' a little indecent about your—

MAE:

Like a slow-motion football tackle—

MARGARET:

Big Daddy's got on his Chinese slippers that I gave him, Brick. Big Daddy, I haven't given you my big present yet, but now I will, now's the time for me to present it to you! I have an announcement to make!

MAE:
What? What kind of announcement?

GOOPER:
A sports announcement, Maggie?

MARGARET:
Announcement of life beginning! A child is coming,
sired by Brick, and out of Maggie the Cat! I have Brick's
child in my body, an' that's my birthday present to Big
Daddy on this birthday!

[*Big Daddy looks at Brick who X behind Big Daddy
to DS portal, L.*]

BIG DADDY:
Get up, girl, get up off your knees, girl.

[*Big Daddy helps Margaret rise. He X above her, to
her R, bites off the end of a fresh cigar, taken from
his bathrobe pocket, as he studies Margaret.*]

Uh-huh, this girl has life in her body, that's no lie!

BIG MAMA:
BIG DADDY'S DREAM COME TRUE!

BRICK:
JESUS!

BIG DADDY [*X R below wicker seat*]:
Gooper, I want my lawyer in the mornin'.

BRICK:
Where are you goin', Big Daddy?

BIG DADDY:
Son, I'm goin' up on the roof to the belvedere on th'
roof to look over my kingdom before I give up my
kingdom—twenty-eight thousand acres of th' richest
land this side of the valley Nile!

[*Exit through R doors, and DR on gallery.*]

BIG MAMA [*following*]:
Sweetheart, sweetheart, sweetheart—can I come with
you?

[*Exits DR.*

[*Margaret is DSC in mirror area.*]

GOOPER [*X to bar*]:
Brick, could you possibly spare me one small shot of that liquor?

BRICK [*DLC*]:
Why, help yourself, Gooper boy.

GOOPER:
I will.

MAE [*X forward*]:
Of course we know that this is a lie!

GOOPER [*drinks*]:
Be still, Mae!

MAE [*X to Gooper at bar*]:
I won't be still! I know she's made this up!

GOOPER:
Goddam it, I said to shut up!

MAE:
That woman isn't pregnant!

GOOPER:
Who said she was?

MAE:
She did.

GOOPER:
The doctor didn't. Doc Baugh didn't.

MARGARET [*X R to above couch*]:
I haven't gone to Doc Baugh.

GOOPER [*X through to L of Margaret*]:
Then who'd you go to, Maggie?
    [*Offstage song finishes.*]

MARGARET:
One of the best gynecologists in the South.

GOOPER:
Uh-huh, I see—

[*Foot on end of couch, trapping Margaret:*]
May we have his name please?

MARGARET:
No, you may not, Mister—Prosecutin' Attorney!

MAE [*X to R of Margaret, above*]:
He doesn't have any name, he doesn't exist!

MARGARET:
He does so exist, and so does my baby, Brick's baby!

MAE:
You can't conceive a child by a man that won't sleep
with you unless you think you're—

    [*Forces Margaret onto couch, turns away C.
    [*Brick starts C for Mae.*]

He drinks all the time to be able to tolerate you! Sleeps
on the sofa to keep out of contact with you!

GOOPER [*X above Margaret, who lies face down on
couch*]:
Don't try to kid us, Margaret—

MAE [*X to bed, L side, rumpling pillows*]:
How can you conceive a child by a man that won't sleep
with you? How can you conceive? How can you? How
can you!

GOOPER [*sharply*]:
MAE!

BRICK [*X below Mae to her R, takes hold of her*]:
Mae, Sister Woman, how d'you know that I don't sleep
with Maggie?

MAE:
We occupy the next room an' th' wall between isn't
soundproof.

BRICK:
Oh . . .

MAE:
We hear the nightly pleadin' and the nightly refusal. So

don't imagine you're goin' t'put a trick over on us, to
fool a dyin' man with—a—

BRICK:
Mae, Sister Woman, not everybody makes much noise
about love. Oh, I know some people are huffers an' puff-
ers, but others are silent lovers.

GOOPER [behind seat, R]:
This talk is pointless, completely.

BRICK:
How d'y'know that we're not silent lovers?
Even if y'got a peep-hole drilled in the wall, how can
y'tell if sometime when Gooper's got business in Memphis an' you're playin' scrabble at the country club with
other ex-queens of cotton, Maggie and I don't come to
some temporary agreement? How do you know that—?
    [He X above wicker seat to above R and couch.]

MAE:
Brick, I never thought that you would stoop to her level,
I just never dreamed that you would stoop to her level.

GOOPER:
I don't think Brick will stoop to her level.

BRICK [sits R of Margaret on couch]:
What is your level? Tell me your level so I can sink or
rise to it.
    [Rises.]
You heard what Big Daddy said. This girl has life in
her body.

MAE:
That is a lie!

BRICK:
No, truth is something desperate, an' she's got it. Believe
me, it's somethin' desperate, an' she's got it.
    [X below seat to below bar.]
An' now if you will stop actin' as if Brick Pollitt was
dead an' buried, invisible, not heard, an' go on back to

your peep-hole in the wall—I'm drunk, and sleepy—not
as alive as Maggie, but still alive. . . .

[*Pours drink, drinks.*]

GOOPER [*picks up briefcase from R foot of bed*]:
Come on, Mae. We'll leave these love birds together in
their nest.

MAE:
Yeah, nest of lice! Liars!

GOOPER:
Mae—Mae, you jes' go on back to our room—

MAE:
Liars!

[*Exits through hall.*]

GOOPER [*DR above Margaret*]:
We're jest goin' to wait an' see. Time will tell.

[*X to R of bar.*]

Yes, sir, little brother, we're just goin' to wait an' see!

[*Exit, hall.*
[*The clock strikes twelve.*
[*Maggie and Brick exchange a look. He drinks
deeply, puts his glass on the bar. Gradually, his ex-
pression changes. He utters a sharp exhalation.*
[*The exhalation is echoed by the singers, off UR, who
commence vocalizing with "Gimme a Cool Drink of
Water Fo' I Die," and continue till end of act.*]

MARGARET [*as she hears Brick's exhalation*]:
The click?

[*Brick looks toward the singers, happily, almost
gratefully. He XR to bed, picks up his pillow, and
starts toward head of couch, DR, Xing above wicker
seat. Margaret seizes the pillow from his grasp, rises,
stands facing C, holding the pillow close. Brick
watches her with growing admiration. She moves
quickly USC, throwing pillow onto bed. She X to
bar. Brick counters below wicker seat, watching her.
Margaret grabs all the bottles from the bar. She goes*

into hall, pitches the bottles, one after the other, off the platform into the UL lawn area. Bottles break, off L. Margaret reenters the room, stands UC, facing Brick.]

Echo Spring has gone dry, and no one but me could drive you to town for more.

BRICK:
Lacey will get me—

MARGARET:
Lacey's been told not to!

BRICK:
I could drive—

MARGARET:
And you lost your driver's license! I'd phone ahead and have you stopped on the highway before you got halfway to Ruby Lightfoot's gin mill. I told a lie to Big Daddy, but we can make that lie come true. And then I'll bring you liquor, and we'll get drunk together, here, tonight, in this place that death has come into! What do you say? What do you say, Baby?

BRICK [*X to L side bed*]:
I admire you, Maggie.

[*Brick sits on edge of bed. He looks up at the over-head light, then at Margaret. She reaches for the light, turns it out; then she kneels quickly beside Brick at foot of bed.*]

MARGARET:
Oh, you weak, beautiful people who give up with such grace. What you need is someone to take hold of you—gently, with love, and hand your life back to you, like something gold you let go of—and I can! I'm determined to do it—and nothing's more determined than a cat on a tin roof—is there? Is there, Baby?

[*She touches his cheek, gently.*]

CURTAIN

About the Author

Tennessee Williams (Thomas Lanier Williams) was born in Columbus, Mississippi, on March 26, 1911, and lived there until he was twelve, when his family moved to St. Louis. His education at the University of Missouri (1931–33) was interrupted for financial reasons, but he later (1938) received his B.A. from the University of Iowa. Tennessee Williams started writing and publishing poetry when very young, while simultaneously holding a variety of jobs—starting with a clerical position in the shoe company that also employed his father. His first real recognition came in 1940 when he received a Rockefeller fellowship and his first play, *Battle of Angels,* was produced by the Theatre Guild in Boston. His first financial break, which enabled him to give full attention to his writing, came with an offer from MGM, which he accepted, abandoning his job as a movie usher. After six months of work in Hollywood, he devoted his time to writing *The Glass Menagerie,* the initial success which established him as one of the leading American playwrights.

Since that time, his plays have been made into movies, produced on TV, turned into operas and ballets—*A Streetcar Named Desire, Summer and Smoke, The Night of the Iguana, Cat on a Hot Tin Roof,* and *The Glass Menagerie,* to name just a few. In May of 1969 Tennessee Williams was awarded the Gold Medal for Literature by the American Academy of Arts and Letters and the National Institute of Arts and Letters. He died on February 25, 1983.

He is the author of the following works: *Baby Doll, Battle of Angels, Camino Real, Cat on a Hot Tin Roof* (winner of the Pulitzer Prize and Drama Critics' Award),

Dragon Country (short plays, including *In the Bar of a Tokyo Hotel*), *The Eccentricities of a Nightingale*, *Eight Mortal Ladies Possessed* (stories), *The Glass Menagerie*, *Hard Candy* (stories), *In the Winter of Cities* (poems), *Kingdom of Earth* (*The Seven Descents of Myrtle*), *The Knightly Quest* (stories), *Memoirs* (autobiography), *The Milk Train Doesn't Stop Here Anymore*, *Moise and the World of Reason* (novel), *The Night of the Iguana* (winner of the Drama Critics' Award), *One Arm & Other Stories*, *Orpheus Descending*, *Out Cry*, *Period of Adjustment*, *The Roman Spring of Mrs. Stone* (novel), *The Rose Tattoo*, *Small Craft Warnings*, *A Streetcar Named Desire* (winner of the Pulitzer Prize and Drama Critics' Award), *Suddenly Last Summer*, *Summer and Smoke*, *Sweet Bird of Youth*, *27 Wagons Full of Cotton*, *The Two-Character Play*, *Vieux Carré*, and *Clothes for a Summer Hotel*.

ACKNOWLEDGMENTS
The quotation from Dylan Thomas is from "Do Not Go Gentle into That Good Night" in *The Collected Poems of Dylan Thomas,* copyright Dylan Thomas, 1952, published by New Directions.

Grateful acknowledgment is made to *The New York Times* Sunday Drama Section in which the article "Person-to-Person" first appeared.

AMERICAN CLASSICS

SPOON RIVER ANTHOLOGY *by Edgar Lee Masters*
with an Introduction by John Hollander and a new Afterword by
Ronald Primeau
A book of dramatic monologues written in free verse about a
fictional town called Spoon River, based on the Midwestern towns
where Edgar Lee Masters grew up.

SELECTED WRITINGS OF
RALPH WALDO EMERSON
with an Introduction by Charles Johnson
Fourteen essays and addresses including *The Oversoul, Politics,*
Thoreau, Divinity School Address, as well as poems *Threnody* and
Uriel, and selections from his letters and journals. Includes Chronology
and Bibliography.

EVANGELINE & Selected Tales and Poems
by Henry Wadsworth Longfellow
Edited by Horace Gregory, with a new introduction by Edward Cifelli
Includes *The Witnesses, The Courtship of Miles Standish,* and
selections from *Hiawatha,* with commentaries on Longfellow by Van
Wyck Brooks, Norman Holmes Pearson, and Lewis Carroll. Includes
Introduction, Bibliography, and Chronology.

WALDEN AND CIVIL DISOBEDIENCE
by Henry David Thoreau
150th Anniversary Edition
Two classic examinations of individuality in relation to nature,
society, and government. *Walden* conveys at once a naturalist's
wonder at the commonplace and a Transcendentalist's yearning for
spiritual truth. "Civil Disobedience," perhaps the most famous essay
in American literature, has inspired activists like Martin Luther King,
Jr. and Gandhi.

Available wherever books are sold or at
signetclassics.com

READ THE TOP 20
SIGNET CLASSICS

1984 BY GEORGE ORWELL

ANIMAL FARM BY GEORGE ORWELL

A STREETCAR NAMED DESIRE BY TENNESSEE WILLIAMS

THE INFERNO BY DANTE

THE ODYSSEY BY HOMER

FRANKENSTEIN BY MARY SHELLEY

NECTAR IN A SIEVE BY KAMALA MARKANDAYA

THE ILIAD BY HOMER

BEOWULF (BURTON RAFFEL, TRANSLATOR)

HAMLET BY WILLIAM SHAKESPEARE

ETHAN FROME BY EDITH WHARTON

NARRATIVE OF THE LIFE OF FREDERICK DOUGLASS
    BY FREDERICK DOUGLASS

THE ADVENTURES OF HUCKLEBERRY FINN BY MARK TWAIN

HEART OF DARKNESS & THE SECRET SHARER
    BY JOSEPH CONRAD

A MIDSUMMER NIGHT'S DREAM BY WILLIAM SHAKESPEARE

WUTHERING HEIGHTS BY EMILY BRONTE

ONE DAY IN THE LIFE OF IVAN DENISOVICH
    BY ALEXANDER SOLZHENITSYN

THE SCARLET LETTER BY NATHANIEL HAWTHORNE

ALICE'S ADVENTURES IN WONDERLAND &
THROUGH THE LOOKING GLASS BY LEWIS CARROLL

A TALE OF TWO CITIES BY CHARLES DICKENS